REDISCOVERING CHRISTIANITY

A Faith for the 21st Century

REDISCOVERING CHRISTIANITY

A Faith for the 21st Century

Dr. Richard Cheatham

Copyright © 2018 by Dr. Richard Cheatham.

Library of Congress Control Number:		2018903741
ISBN:	Hardcover	978-1-9845-1764-7
	Softcover	978-1-9845-1763-0
	eBook	978-1-9845-1762-3

All rights reserved. No part of this book may be reproduced or transmitted in any form or by any means, electronic or mechanical, including photocopying, recording, or by any information storage and retrieval system, without permission in writing from the copyright owner.

Scripture quotations marked NIV are taken from the Holy Bible, New International Version®. NIV®. Copyright © 1973, 1978, 1984 by International Bible Society. Used by permission of Zondervan. All rights reserved. [Biblica]

Any people depicted in stock imagery provided by Getty Images are models, and such images are being used for illustrative purposes only. Certain stock imagery © Getty Images.

Print information available on the last page.

Rev. date: 03/26/2018

To order additional copies of this book, contact:
Xlibris
1-888-795-4274
www.Xlibris.com
Orders@Xlibris.com
775555

CONTENTS

Introduction xiii

Section 1: Deism versus Christianity 1

Section 2: Scripture 11

Section 3: Theology 28

Section 4: Monotheism versus Henotheism 42

Section 5: Biblical Errors 53

Section 6: Questionable Doctrines 66

Section 7: So Where Now? 106

PREFACE

The first great heresy of the church was to take the faith *of* Jesus and transform it into a religion *about* Jesus. He was not attempting to create a new faith or regenerate an existing one. Jesus did not conduct worship services. He was a teacher. He taught people how to live lives pleasing to God. He had two basic themes:

1. God is a loving parent who wants to be in relationship with us.
2. We are to treat one another with kindness. The early followers of Jesus developed their lives on those messages. They created a community that cared for one another in profound ways. They transcended normal boundaries to be inclusive. They proclaimed God as having compassion, justice, and empowerment. It was liberating for them and gave deeper meaning to their personal lives.

Somewhere along the line, the focus of the faith moved from concern for others to concern for the self. "Have you been saved?" was the crucial issue. With egocentricity as its base, the faith took off in a multitude of directions: some worthy and some destructive. My purpose in writing this book is to help serious spiritual pilgrims understand the faith proclaimed by Jesus and to find ways to recover that liberating, empowering faith in their own lives.

ACKNOWLEDGMENTS

I often have reason to recall the words of Tennyson: "I am a part of all that I have met." When I begin to write the acknowledgements for a book, I become increasingly aware of the innumerable encounters that have contributed to my understanding. Dr. Samuel Laeuchli, my professor of church history, must be near the head of the list. He did not teach us church history. He guided us in developing the skills to *do* church history. There is a world of difference between the two. He also gave us the freedom to explore anything written to ascertain whether it was valid and to understand why those events were selected to be told. Without the experience of Dr. Laeuchli, there could be no book of this ilk.

I would be remiss if I did not include Dr. Al Sundberg in my list of mentors. He was a professor of the New Testament, who, in spite of the brilliance of his mind, was down to earth and humble. I was aware of his contributions as I wrote some of the lessons he imparted.

I met John Biersdorf at the right time in my journey. This nation was just awakening to an awareness of its spiritual hunger. Pentecostal groups were erupting across the land.

Eastern spiritualism was being imported, even though it did not match the psyche of the Western mind. John had been attuned to this long before others became aware of their hunger. He had researched and developed a spiritual path that suited at least this Western mind. John helped set my feet upon that path and gave enough guidance for me to find my way alone. His guidance has added immensely to the richness of my journey and allowed some of the insights I have garnered along the way.

Open-minded parishioners who hungered for greater understanding kept me encouraged and current in my research. Good, inquisitive minds are a blessing to any pastor. The adult class, named Seekers at University United Methodist Church in San Antonio, was especially helpful and confirming with this book. They read the manuscript even as it was being written. Their observations, suggestions, and encouragement were extremely helpful.

I will mention one family from the Birmingham United Methodist Church in Michigan, Gary and Margaret Valade. Their encouragement and support were vital in the writing and publication of this book. During a hospital visit where I was undergoing a serious medical issue, Margaret read the introduction and immediately told me the book would be excellent. When I finally recovered enough to reenter the world, I found the pages I had written and decided to spend recovery time doing something useful.

My daughters—Deborah, Cynthia, and Crystal—are my constant rooting section that allows me to believe I can write words worth reading. This brings me to my biggest booster, Diane—my perpetual bride, best friend, and life partner.

She believes in me more than I merit, and she does the basic editing and proofreading my works always require.

Throw in literally hundreds of individuals who touched me in particular ways, and you have the list. "I am a part of all that I have met."

Richard Cheatham, March 1, 2018

INTRODUCTION

This book was inspired by an attractive young preacher who was persuasive in his preaching skills. He held the congregation's attention, and I could see them nodding in approval as he spoke. There was only one problem: his theology was out of line with reality. Unwittingly, he was leading his listeners astray.

It may not have been his fault. It possibly was the failure of the seminary to provide him with the proper education. There are two primary reasons for this: (1) There are seminaries today that attract those who were raised in churches pastored by clergy who had been taught an outdated theology. No matter how sincere they may be, they no longer address the reality of the world in which we live. They simply perpetuate a view that is no longer relevant to the present. (2) Ministry today requires too many skills for the seminaries to teach in three or four years. When I attended seminary, the degree given was a BD (bachelor of divinity). Today, the same degree is now called an MDiv (master of divinity). What I received was at a basic level. I realized I was going to be assigned to a church still lacking the skills I believed were required to lead my congregation properly. That is why I remained to complete a doctorate. My major professor technically taught church history. However, he was qualified to teach history, historical theology, systematic theology, and the New Testament at the doctoral level, and he combined them all for his doctoral students. Additionally, what he did not know about art and architecture was not worth knowing. We spent time at the Chicago Art Institute, understanding the change in the human psyche that brought about the Renaissance and the ensuing Reformation and Enlightenment. We emerged with our degrees, understanding not only the movement of history but also the underlying human dynamics that generated them.

The other reason the truth is not proclaimed from the pulpit might be fear. Many preachers fear the reaction of conservative members if they proclaim a theology different from the one they learned as a child in Sunday school. From both first- and secondhand experiences, I know this to be true.

My reason for writing this is to give some factual information to those who wish to understand the roots of our faith grounded in the life of Jesus Christ and the early writings of his followers. I believe the church has coasted as far as it can on outdated beliefs and creeds. Rather than just change the form of our faith, we need to change the content—to restore the powerful message it held that allowed the church to survive and thrive in a world that feared its truth.

I do not claim that what I am offering is the purest expression of the faith. I make no claim of being a great theologian. What I am offering is the understanding I have acquired over a lifetime of ministry. I will support my ideas with Scripture, reason, historical perspectives, and personal experience. I realize there are many people who will disagree with my thinking, and I readily accept that—if they also will support their ideas with the same intellectual tools. The Christian faith is a universal religion. It necessarily will find many worthy forms of expression. These essays are for those who are seeking theirs but have not yet found one that resonates with them. I also intend to incorporate from a variety of the academic disciplines that are a part of our collective experience.

A Contemporary Approach to Rediscovering the Message and Faith of Jesus Christ

I want to make it quite clear at the start that the changes that have altered the original message were honest attempts to clarify or expand on the original message. Those that endured were formulated by high-quality minds who were limited by the existing understandings of their time. Some of these, once formulated, were corrupted by lesser men for lesser purposes. Sometimes the theologians were outstanding philosophical thinkers but poor biblical scholars. We shall deal with them as they naturally arise in this writing.

There are certain assumptions that must be stated and clarified in the process. The first concerns the origin of the universe: it either had a beginning or it always existed. For no other reason than it seems more logical, I assume the universe has a beginning. For me, this allows for a prior, nonphysical cause and thus a nonphysical realm beyond our grasp.

The next assumption concerns whether there was a purpose or the act of Creation was random. Again, for no other reason than I believe it to be more logical, I assume the act of Creation was purposeful.

A third assumption concerns the origin of humanity. Again, I assume that humanity is an intentional and meaningful part of Creation. This leads to the question of the purpose served by humanity. We certainly do not contribute to the continuing development of the universe. We also do not contribute to the well-being of the planet we call Earth. The natural environment has been disrupted solely because of the presence of humanity, caring for itself. What possible purpose can humanity serve in our present state? Many times, I find my mind drifting to a poem by James Weldon Johnson. He took the basic tale found in Genesis 1 and crafted it into a lovely folk poem. *"I'm lonely. I think I will make me a world."* If the long-stated assumption about the nature of God is agape love, then it follows that the creative force we call God requires something or someone to love. There is a saying in the Jewish Talmud that *man's task is to know God and to enjoy Him forever.* For me, this is in keeping with my assumption that humanity's task is to love and be loved by God.

I do not understand a judgmental, punishing deity who condemns people for being who they are. I believe my statement on heaven and hell will clearly express my thoughts on that.

Now I want to switch gears, as it were, and make some assumptions in a different direction.

We have learned that there are inflexible physical principles of the universe. No one breaks them. People either learn them and adjust to them or are hindered or injured by them. The principles are stated as laws. The law of gravity is an obvious example. The laws of health are another. Certain foods and activities are harmful. Others are helpful. A person may ignore the rules but only at one's peril. People and cultures who opt for a healthy lifestyle tend to live longer and have fewer illnesses. That is obvious and undeniable.

Just as there are inflexible physical principles, I believe there also are inflexible moral/ethical principles. The goal of philosophers and theologians is to learn these principles and to share them with the public. This is where I believe many religions go astray. The use of enticements or terror to guide a group simply is not productive. The expressions of belief in the superiority of a particular belief system also is not helpful. Comparative goodness only serves to generate a useless sense of superiority and complacency. I had the good fortune of teaching world religions at the university level a few decades ago. The research and ensuing classes opened me to a wider and fresher understanding of the various faith expressions we call religions. When we delve beneath the surface, we discover a greater commonality than diversity in the faiths. For years, I have served on the worship committee that develops the ecumenical service for the Martin Luther King celebration in San Antonio, Texas. Frankly, I find I have more in common with the mixed-faith group than I have with many in my own United Methodist congregation.

The members possess a spirit of generosity and openness that is uplifting.

All expressions of these moral/ethical laws, unfortunately, must be made in the cultural context of those who receive them. Consequently, they reflect the long-established beliefs of those people. At this point, I want to introduce the term *moral/ethical principles*. Underlying every moral/ethical law is a fundamental principle. These principles are the basis for all moral/ethical laws developed by the various cultures.

The rediscovery of Christianity may prove far more dramatic than you would wish or even believe. The struggle throughout its history has been the duel between our human dimension and our spiritual dimension. I have long-claimed that we are not mere humans who occasionally have a spiritual experience. Rather we are spiritual beings presently undergoing a physical experience.

Bear with me, and I will give my reasons for this belief: I believe I will get no argument that prior to what scientists call the big bang and religionists might call the beginning, there was neither time nor space. What existed was a realm of the spirit or spiritual energy or just plain energy that did not require space for its existence. Both time and space, incidentally, have been proven to have no constant value. I therefore contend that they do not have absolute existence. Their dimensions and movement are determined by relative factors. Our brains developed in the arena of time and space, and as a result, we have no ability to understand a form of existence without it. Yet logic demands that there must be a timeless, spaceless realm prior to the universe in which we presently live. You and I are not even capable of comprehending a spaceless realm. Yet scientists assure us that space is expanding at an ever-increasing rate of speed. When we try to comprehend it, our mind only allows us to perceive an empty space—never a spaceless realm. It simply is beyond our comprehension.

So I say our source and final destination (eternity) lies within the realm of spacelessness. Ergo we must be primarily beings of that realm.

The Primary Rules by Which I Do My Theology

1. Ockham's razor—this simply means that the simplest answer is probably the correct answer. Rather than constructing a contorted explanation to explain a process, the least complicated is the desired—and most likely—explanation.
2. My functional definition of *truth* is this: it is the hypothesis that successfully answers every question posed to it. If a question arises that cannot be answered by that hypothesis, then that understanding of truth is no longer functional. If a person chooses to deny the legitimate questions posed by this scientifically oriented society, I assume that person has chosen to remain intentionally ignorant. Any discussion with that person will only prove to be frustrating—never fruitful.
3. Check the premises. Every decision we make is based upon at least one premise. Most of our premises are long-accepted, assumed truths. We begin our

reasoning process by unconsciously accepting certain long-held truths and proceeding from there. I have learned that many false conclusions are logically attained through this process. The old adage "What goes up must come down" no longer is true in this day of space venturing. We now realize that it is possible to overcome the operational force of gravity that once made this an unquestionable truth. As you will read a bit further into this book, you will see that a few false premises are the root cause of the doctrine of Trinity. Without those, that doctrine no longer serves a purpose but—at least in my estimation—interferes with the search for truth.

4. Try to discern God's purpose in any of his actions. We always will fall short of doing this, but it is a good starting point when doing theology. Draw from John Wesley's quadrilateral of Scripture, tradition, reason, and experience in this attempt.

SECTION 1

DEISM VERSUS CHRISTIANITY

As I write this book, I am well aware that there are essentially two diverse theological groups. We broadly call them *Conservative* or *Evangelical* and *Contemporary* or *Liberal*. Until the last two hundred years, those terms had no meaning and were not used to identify Christians. The Enlightenment changed that. It ushered in the era of scientific investigation. Prior to that time, people passively accepted the worldview of the book of Genesis and assumed Scripture was the primary source of ultimate truth. The scientific method demanded empirical evidence before accepting anything as fact. Newton presented an entirely new universe, one that made mathematical sense and presented the opportunity for exploration and understanding. A latent question in any discussion of the universe was the nature of whatever—or whoever—created and sustains it. For the first time, scholars began to pore over Scripture with a critical eye. They accepted the universe of Newton and studied the Scriptures from that perspective. Eventually, a school of theology calling itself higher criticism emerged, calling into question long-assumed beliefs.

Higher criticism possessed intellectual tools unavailable to previous generations. Linguistic analysis allowed scholars to recognize the difference in authorship of the various writings. The in-depth study of early writings allowed the scholars to understand that myths, parables, and legends were legitimate—and common—motifs for communicating wisdom rather than facts. There was an increasing acceptance in the understanding that there was no magical period when the early authors of Scripture were more carefully guided in their writings.

With these new tools, the more highly educated "intellectuals" redefined Christianity into a form they called Deism. They continued to call themselves Christians but radically redefined the theology. They perceived Jesus as a great moral teacher and never demeaned his role as a teacher and example for humanity. However, they viewed the Creator God as more of an absentee landlord than a benevolent parent constantly watching over his children. They discarded miracles as wishful fantasies and coined the term *the best of all worlds*. They reasoned that a benevolent deity would not create a world that was less than the best that could be created. If this world was the best possible, then any disruption by miracle was unnecessary. The world as it operated was the best; therefore, no miracle could improve upon the overall plan.

There has been great debate over whether the founding fathers of our nation intended to establish a Christian nation. Conservatives say, "Yes," while Liberals say, "No, they did not." Conservatives claim that the founding fathers were Christians, while the more Liberal element claims they were primarily Deists. You might employ the term Christian Deists, but the difference is significant.

Let's look at a few of the more influential founding fathers:

1. Thomas Paine was influential because of his writings. His *Age of Reason* was a best seller. Many may recall learning of this work while in high school. What they probably did not learn was that it was a Deist polemic against organized religion. The fact that it was a best seller should say something about those who purchased copies. The educated class purchased most of the books of that era. They had more time and discretionary cash for such luxuries. It therefore seems reasonable to assume that Deism had at least a strong influence upon the civilian leadership of the time. Remember, it was a best seller. Many were influenced by its thought.

2. Thomas Jefferson had a problem with a state or national religion. Virginia was one of the few states in which a single expression of faith (Anglicanism) was established as the only proper faith. Taxes were raised to pay church expenses, and an article even claimed that if a person was not of the Anglican faith, then that person was unfit for public service. One of Jefferson's greatest accomplishments, he believed, was to enact the Articles of Religious Freedom for Virginia, thereby ending the practice of an established church.

Jefferson wrote his own understanding of the role of Jesus as a teacher of a strong moral religion. It was the teachings and actions of Jesus as recorded in the Gospel accounts—minus any mention of miracles. He openly denied the divinity of Jesus and the doctrine of the Trinity. Read the Declaration of Independence, and you will find not a trace of Jesus Christ. Rather, Jefferson believed in a divine providence that might best be expressed in Romans 8:28: "We know that in all things God works for the good with those who love him and are called according to his purpose."

3. John Adams claimed to be Unitarian, as did his wife, Abigail. This automatically eliminated the divinity of Jesus and doctrine of the Trinity. Unitarians may (or may not) think of themselves as Christians in that they believe Jesus actually was the anointed one of God. They see him as the example of humanity he was called to become, but that is as far as they will go.

Adams took public exception to Paine's writings. He decried his mocking of Christianity, believing it to be the highest moral authority essentially for the preservation of any state. He also attended church regularly. He feared any direct tie between religion and government, believing it corrupted the church, and he also fought for a balance of power between the three governmental branches: legislative, executive, and judiciary. He seemed to understand the inherent weakness in humanity that sought power.

Adams is not easy to describe, except to say he was Unitarian and did not want any religion to be in control of the nation.

4. George Washington was too politically astute to be able to properly evaluate his faith. When in a public setting, he attended church services with great regularity. However, at home, he was far less regular. He was careful of his public statements, so careful in fact that it seemed staged. He obviously set the character of a Christian for anyone who considered himself to be a patriot. But that said nothing of his actual belief system. We are not certain if he ever was baptized. At his death, he did not ask for a clergyman.

5. Ben Franklin was another founding father who understood the importance of a strong moral fiber sustaining the citizenship of a functional democracy. Just prior to his death, he agreed to write a summary of his faith. There were two main points: Unless a religion serves to increase the virtue of its adherents, it is a worthless waste. And Jesus the Christ was the greatest moral teacher, but he was not divine.

In his later youth, Franklin read the argument for Deism and decided he was a Deist. He never retreated from that position. He also once made the statement that the world was filed with weak and ignorant men and women who needed a religion that would keep them striving to be better. By scanning his works over the years, it is easy to see that if a religion helped to shape a better moral character in a person, then it was acceptable. He never expressed a personal concern about salvation. This traditional focus of Christianity was never a part of his thinking.

A common thread among these early shapers of our nation seems to be a need for the separation of church and state. Another common thread was the admiration of Jesus as a great moral teacher—but not divine. The primary value of a religion was its ability to shape a moral society that represented the best Judaic/Christian virtues.

Unitarianism, incidentally, was developed from a search to understand and dismiss the idea of predestination (the concept that one was destined either for heaven or hell from birth). It found its way into denying Trinitarian doctrine as a by-product of that search. It also was the natural consequence of the Enlightenment.

Colonial Deism was an early response to the understandings that rose from the Enlightenment. Today, a form of Deism runs through most of Liberal Christianity. A believer might accept the stories of Jesus's healings but reject the more dramatic ones as inconsistent with their understanding of nature—and unnecessary additions to an otherwise rational tale. The fact that most of the founding fathers attended Christian churches should not be taken as proof of a belief in traditional Christianity.

My first awareness of the Deism within me came in a discussion with a professor who exclaimed, "You would make a great Unitarian minister." I responded that I could not be a Unitarian because I believed Jesus is the Christ. "So do I!" the Unitarian professor responded. "I just do not believe he is God." I sat silent for a moment, trying to process what I had heard. I never had thought in terms of Jesus being God or equal to God. I had grown up singing the hymn "Holy, holy, holy. God in three persons blessed Trinity." Frankly, I had never thought about the implications of God in three persons. I realized the universe was billions of light-years in its age and size. The thought that a person—no matter how outstanding—could be responsible for creating and maintaining that never occurred to me.

If I had thought about it, I would have rationalized that people tended to objectify a subjective opinion: "That was a great movie" equals "I liked it." "He is the greatest singer of the present time" equals "I like him best." I thought of Jesus as God focused. In him, we see all we are capable—or needful—of understanding about God's will and nature. To add to that, everything Jesus said about his relationship to God suggested that God was by far the superior in rank.

As I reflected upon that conversation, I began to realize that we had taken the faith *of* Jesus and converted it into a faith *about* Jesus. Contrary to scriptural evidence, we had decided to make Jesus into God. At seminary, my doctoral specialties were the development of Christology and the doctrine of the Trinity. I had to understand why and how Jesus had become God in the minds of followers. With that transformation—from human to divine—an entirely new and unsupported doctrine emerged. With that change, I believe we lost the essence of Jesus Christ's message.

When I approach that subject, it may cause the reader to feel uncomfortable being asked to examine and possibly abandon long-held beliefs. If you follow my explanation and evidence, however, I believe it will give a fresher, more meaningful understanding to your faith.

This book is not for Conservative Christians. I know many Conservative Christians who are loyal followers of Jesus Christ. They are loving, generous spirits. However, their system demands a world that is inconsistent with today's world. Beliefs are transitory. Nature is inflexible. As a result, they make decisions based upon mythology and legend rather than scientifically established fact. This false worldview, in turn, causes them to make improper and often unfortunate choices on issues of health, environment, and human relations. Much bigotry has been given the blessings of the church because of beliefs from a faraway time.

This book is written for those who still are seeking greater and clearer understanding. It is my sincere hope that those who read this carefully, thoughtfully, and reflectively will find new pathways to an increasingly closer relationship to our Creator, Sustainer God.

I ask that you carefully read the Gospel to see if there is any suggestion that Jesus believed God is alienated from his children. Also, see if you can define in a few words what you believe Jesus is trying to accomplish with his teachings and practices. Then compare what you have learned with the present teachings and proclamations of the church.

Also read both Matthew and Luke for the same understanding. Aside from a throwaway line that Matthew puts in Jesus's mouth ("for the forgiveness of sins" in 26:28), there is no hint in any of the Gospel accounts that God feels the need for an act of sacrifice in order to be reconciled with his people.

I do not want to suggest that I am offering the only correct way to interpret Scripture or understand doctrine. We were given the Scriptures but without any instructions as to how they should be interpreted. At various points in our history, church councils gathered and agreed upon certain teachings (doctrines). As one who has sat through many church conferences, I have some idea of how resolutions are formulated and enacted. I can safely say that none of the resolutions are, or ever were, sacrosanct. I think of the doctrines as being the best expression of an understanding of the faith *that could be formulated at the time*. Doctrines, like laws, need to be updated regularly in order to remain relevant to the culture.

I also do not mean to suggest that these essays present the only true expression of our Christian faith. There is not one true expression of our faith. What I am offering is an alternative means for understanding the faith for those who have not found an expression of faith that resonates within them, is acceptable to their minds, and serves their needs. What I offer is based upon the scholarship acquired through my doctoral studies and more than fifty years of active, reflective ministry.

My doctorial focus was in patristics (study of the early church). I believed the church had made many shortsighted doctrinal decisions in their attempt to create a unified faith. Unfortunately, these decisions were given the stamp of approval by some church council and became written in stone—unable to change with the changing understanding and culture. As a consequence, we find it difficult today to define precisely what constitutes being a Christian.

I simply am sharing the understandings that contemporary scholarship has accepted but that far too few seminary students have the time, opportunity, or inclination to acquire. I sincerely believe that it is possible to have a lay revival by intelligent, informed laity that can awaken the original spirit and purpose of the early followers of Jesus. In doing this, I believe we can arrive at a clearer, more relevant understanding of the purpose of humanity in God's plan and a much clearer understanding of ourselves and our life purpose.

SECTION 2

SCRIPTURE

Since Scripture is the primary source of our faith, we will spend much time exploring Scripture from a variety of perspectives. Unfortunately, there was not a smooth developmental process that we can look at sequentially. As a consequence, what I shall offer is an amalgamation of various themes related to the development and canonization of Scripture.

The school of higher criticism, by analyzing the writing of Scripture, became aware that there were a number of writers contributing to the so-called Books of Moses. Further analysis disclosed that many of the Scriptures were written hundreds of years after the reported events. Each era has its special language. The vocabulary and syntax evolve in a living language. One has only to watch the older movies on television to see this. If, for example, the term *swell* is used to denote something pleasant or good, you can be sure you are seeing a movie from the '40s. Terms like *interface* did not appear until the '80s. This always has been the pattern of a living language. Words change their meanings; old words disappear, and new ones appear. Scholars had only to do some research to discover and systematize that. Once this tool was developed, any open-minded scholar would see Scripture in its historical perspective.

This challenge to scriptural authority caused a defensive backlash. There always are those who feel a need to defend long-held beliefs. It was at this time that the church made the tragic mistake of separating science and religion. Rather than incorporating the findings and techniques of science into their faith, they chose to deny what they believed to be an attack on their authority. That separation continues to exist in the camp we call Conservative or Evangelical.

Back in the 1970s, Erich Fromm published a book titled *To Have or to Be*. Fromm claims that people make an unconscious decision either to live in the security mode or the becoming mode. People in *the security mode* are those who must possess or have. This includes the realm of ideas or beliefs. Those in the *becoming mode* can let go of whatever offers security in order to become more of what they believe they are called to become. Jesus called people to live in the *becoming mode*. He challenged people to give themselves in service in order to find life abundant.

When Paul began to translate the Jewish-oriented message for the Western culture, he had to use terms relevant to their culture in order to be understood. The Western culture at the time was heavily influenced by Roman law and Stoic philosophy, which placed emphasis on natural law. As a consequence, Western Christians began to think of themselves as either guilty or not guilty, saved or lost. Over a period of time, being saved became the goal, and the faith slipped into the security side of the ledger. Church leaders who were elders and deacons for their wisdom and servanthood became priests who stood between laity and deity, dispensing salvation. Eventually, they rose to positions of great power and wealth. They accomplished this in such a slow and normal-appearing manner that few seemed to notice the change. What was most notable to me was the change in the values and goals of the leadership. During the period when the church had to struggle and sacrifice in order to survive, the leadership was made up of those who were willing to struggle and sacrifice. They saw themselves as servant people, called to care for the needy. When Constantine declared the faith as the faith of the empire, the leadership became a position of power and privilege. These were the qualities that sought and attained church leadership positions. At one point, wealthy nobility made contributions to the proper church authorities to ensure that their younger sons would become bishops. A decent episcopal see could provide a quality of life suitable for wealthy young nobility. This transition, although begun early, required a few centuries to become a standard practice for appointing bishops.

At this point, I need to insert some understanding from the school of psychology called typology. The complete description of psychological types covers sixteen basic types of personality. However, they group together in such a manner that one may fairly well define them by four basic types: SJ, SP, NF, and NT. The *S* denotes *sensing* as the dominant quality. Sensors receives data primarily through the five senses. They know what they see, smell, touch, taste, and hear. They tend to be the practical, pragmatic, no-nonsense people. The *J* denotes the judging type. *J*s prefer to arrive at a decision quickly. They garner what they believe to be sufficient information to make a decision. They make it and move on. The *P* denotes the perceptive type, who is content to perceive information until it is necessary to make a decision. We all have overheard—and been in—conversations that ran this way:

"You don't know that."

"It should be obvious."

"I agree it looks that way, but we don't have enough data to be certain."

"I think we do."

"I think you're jumping to conclusions."

The two will never agree because their difference in type causes their reactions.

Now, let's add the *N, F, T* factors. The *N* denotes an intuitor. (Yes, it should start with an *I*, but the letter *I* is already used in denoting an introvert.) Intuitors do not have the great concern for what is but for what the possibilities and underlying principles are. They are not good at details but tend to be more analytical. They began to rely upon their intuition at an early age, and so they tend to be far more intuitive than the more pragmatic sensors. In any conversation, it is not difficult to discern if the speaker is more concerned with facts than ideas.

F denotes the feeling type. To suggest that the feeler only chooses the good feeling over the reasonable option would be a mistake. The feeler is just more attuned to the effect of any decision upon other people. A more accurate term might be *valuer*, for the feeler is concerned with the value being discussed more than the reasonableness of an action. A simple way to determine a feeler from a thinker (*T*) is to see what choice a person makes when the choice is between head and heart. The *T*—of course, as thinker—immediately relies upon logic. Actually, the difference can be resolved among these two because both types accept values and logic as reasonable criteria for decision-making. Types denote preferences. It never is an either/or choice.

Now, having given some basic understanding of this profoundly useful tool, I will explain that *S*s outnumber *N*s by three to one. This means they will almost always be the majority group. SJ personalities like routines, rules, and guidelines. They feel most comfortable with the familiar. This is completely unrelated to security needs, incidentally. At their best, SJs are the salt-of-the-earth, dependable friends that make our society work as well as it does. This tendency to want order and routine, however, causes them to package the original dynamic of a faith in a user-friendly manner. They were the good people of biblical times who slowly transformed the order of Jewish religious life into a set of rules—laws.

They also are the good people who took the freeing message of Jesus and turned it into canon law. In doing so, they transformed the elders and deacons of their faith fellowship into priests who stood as authorities somewhere between the people and God. Without concern for the words of the Scripture (1 Peter 2:5) that wrote of the priesthood of all believers, the office of priest snuck in through the backdoor and became the norm. Peter traveled with Jesus throughout his ministry. He, more than anyone else, understood the mind of his master. The book of Mark is based on his memories as recorded by his nephew who traveled with him for years.

Throughout these presentations, I hope the reader will realize and appreciate the fact that the early church fathers were good people sincerely trying to do their best to pass along the message of Christ. They just did not have the intellectual tools, the right organization, and the experience to do a thoroughly accurate job. What developed over a period of time was a hodgepodge of practices and beliefs that slowly moved away from the message of Jesus Christ and became more the reflection of a few that were grounded in their personal struggles and understandings of their culture. Does any sane person today believe Jesus would have approved of Paul's command: "*Slaves, obey your masters*"? (Colossians 3:22, Ephesians 6:5). Just as the colonial church used those passages of Scripture to justify their enslavement of other humans, there are those today who use words of Scripture Jesus never would have endorsed to justify their bigotry against other fellow humans.

There was no central authority for the first few centuries of the church's existence. Antioch and Alexandria were the two most significant churches—and bishops. The two eventually split into what we today call the Roman Catholic Church and the Eastern Orthodox Church. Along the way, a series of exceptionally skilled bishops seated in Rome became mediators for these two factions. Eventually, the slogan "Look to Rome for leadership" became an accepted understanding, and the seat of the Western church moved to Rome. Eventually, Rome claimed authority by citing the statement found in Matthew 16:18, which can be construed to proclaim Peter as the head of the church. However, here are some major problems in accepting that Jesus actually proclaimed Peter to be his successor. A careful reading of the book of Acts should make it clear that James, the brother of Jesus, was the head of the Jerusalem Church. Further, a careful reading of Paul's letter to the Romans reveals that in his many greetings to leaders in the church there, he never mentioned Peter. Since he obviously wishes to show the various ties he has with them, it is unthinkable that he would have ignored sending a greeting to their bishop. Additionally, the early leaders of the Roman Church were called *presiders*—not *bishops*. Nevertheless, the understanding of Peter as the first bishop of Rome is too entrenched in the Catholic psyche to waste time trying to set that straight. In light of today's understandings, priorities, and needs, it matters little at all.

It is critical that today's Bible student and/or scholar keeps in mind that no matter how sincere they were, the early writers (such as Paul, Peter, and John) were not the Messiah. *They were interpreters of the Messiah as they had known him.* Peter and John wrote of the historic Jesus. Paul never encountered the historic Jesus, but he wrote of his experience of the risen Christ. Like any faithful interpreter, early writers drew from their understanding to make statements that were directed to the needs and understandings of their audiences. Their words never—*never*—should be given the same value as those attributed to Jesus. When they run counter to what we know about Jesus, those writings should be discounted and understood to be culturally grounded thoughts.

Another View

Every major religion has its collection of writings, and they may have been attributed to the founder or hero of that religion. Over a period of time, they are seen as authoritative. When we move away from the founding heroes, we seek some certainty that what continues follows the same path as the founders. The Jewish Scriptures followed this pattern. However, their earliest writings have been lost to us except for being mentioned as primary sources in the writings drawn from them.

The oldest and most venerated of the Jewish Scriptures are that group known as the Books of Moses, or the Pentateuch. The next section in importance contain the writings of the prophets. In the Gospel accounts, Jesus refers to them as the law and the prophets. The other section was not accepted as authoritative until after the fall of Jerusalem in 70 CE. Unfortunately for the Jewish faith, the decision was then to close the canon (authoritative writings) for all time. The reason for this seems to be based on two factors:

1. The Jews realized they were being exiled from Jerusalem by the very durable Roman Empire. This would last a considerable time, so it was important that the acceptable Scriptures be recognized. Since this dispersion would be lengthy, an acceptable canon of new writings would be difficult to achieve.
2. Perhaps more pressing was the awareness that a new offshoot Jewish sect was rising that claimed the Messiah had already arrived. Many of their writings

were circulating. Many of those writings are in the collection known as the Books of the New Testament. In order to keep them from becoming authoritative, it was best to close the Jewish canon permanently.

An array of writings from the people who called themselves the People of the Way began circulating indiscriminately. Many claimed apostolic authorship. Some had value, but some were pure fantasy. One account, for instance, stated that when Jesus was but a young lad, he got into a dispute with a neighboring boy, cursed the boy, and the boy fell dead. The author probably thought he was enhancing the power of Jesus even before his baptism, but the story is horrendous.

An early school on biblical studies developed in Alexandria near the end of the first century by a brilliant young nineteen-year-old scholar named Origen. He proposed that Scripture should be read for its historic, moral, and spiritual message. Others proposed similar theories, and the school of Alexandria became an early day leader in biblical scholarship.

The term *bible* is derived from the city of Biblos, which was famous for its library. Scripture developed long before the advent of the printing press, so a collection of scrolls constituted what we call the Holy Bible. As with any library, the books were a mixture of history, inspirational writings, poetry, biographies, dramas, mythology, legends, and fiction that imparted wisdom and understanding. Anyone understanding this can easily discern the various books, particularly from the Jewish Bible that fit these categories.

At this point, I will explain the technical meaning of two categories of writings that often are misunderstood: myth and legend.

A myth is a tale that might not have historical basis but is designed to express an idea larger than the story itself. We have two creation myths, for example. One is designed to affirm the goodness of Creation, including humanity. The other attempts to explain how sin, sickness, and death came to be realities of life. Myths are not meant to be understood as historically true. Most myths have too many logical errors to hold up under scrutiny.

Myths may be stories that are designed to impart understanding rather than mere facts. Understanding—or wisdom—was far more important to the Jewish mind than mere facts. Wisdom is that attribute that allows us to grow from experience and observation. Wisdom, accumulated over time, develops a life that has learned to deal comfortably with the events of life. Wisdom informs us as to what differences to accept and what differences to resist. Wisdom teaches patience and the ability to reflect and analyze the events of life prior to determining their value and purpose.

I do not believe wisdom can be taught. Facts can be taught. Wisdom must be acquired. Secondhand wisdom is merely a collection of advice on how to behave or react in a given situation. The advice columnists who answer the many questions about life are an example of secondhand-wisdom dispensers. The people they help can never acquire enough wisdom to make their own decisions. Wisdom can only be acquired experientially after a time of reflection. The good news is that the experience does not have to be endured personally. It might be vicarious. We all have had the experience of leaving a theater—or putting down a novel—realizing we have gained a fresh understanding or perspective on life. We also may have had the experience of working closely with someone who has undergone a life-changing event. The wisdom acquired may not be so profound as the wisdom acquired by the participant. Still, we realize we have learned a lesson about ourselves or some life characteristic that is significant.

Jesus was a master teacher. As such, he also would have been a master storyteller. He could dispense wisdom in one-liners, as with the Sermon on the Mount or through his parables. He would have had the skill to draw his listeners into the story in such a way that they were vicariously involved and related to the characters. I think of the parables as minimyths created by Jesus. On one of my visits to Israel, our group was taken to the site of the inn of which Jesus spoke in the tale we call the Good Samaritan. The building was—at most—five hundred years old. Yet this was a part of the tour that was experienced by thousands of faithful pilgrims every year. I challenged the guide as to the authenticity of the building, but he held his ground, insisting that this comparatively modern edifice was genuine. All the while, faithful pilgrims snapped the shutter on their cameras, recording their visit. In my mind, the parables were woven out of Jesus's fertile imagination as a means of imparting understanding—wisdom about God's will and ways. In this regard, I should spend a moment explaining the role of storytellers in the first century. Good storytellers were in demand during that era. The evenings were long and often boring. A storyteller entered a village and became the equivalent of a circus coming to town in the early twentieth century. He told carefully crafted tales in serial form. Some lasted for months, much like miniseries television shows. They gave people something to think about during their work hours and something to talk about at the table or while doing chores. Just as people today relate to certain characters, they related to the principal actors in the spoken stories. By the time the story ended, the listeners had developed strong empathy with many of the characters in the tale. What we read in the Gospel accounts as parables are only the very sketchy outline and punch line.

I imagine that during the story of the prodigal son, there were many occasions when Jesus spoke of the father—looking at the empty chair, staring out of the window, or standing to stretch while in the field and gazing down the road to see if possibly his son had returned. The listeners would have felt the sorrow and concern of the father. Then one day, as he stretched himself and gazed down the road, he saw a distant figure walking with what was a familiar stride. He watched for a long moment until he was certain. Then he dropped his trowel and began to walk toward the road. His steps increased in speed, and the distance narrowed until both could see the other clearly. The son began his rehearsed speech, but the father ignored it and embraced his son warmly, crying out for all to hear, "My son has come home!" The parable may have lasted six weeks, complete with false hopes, hidden tears, and episodes of the older brother pushing himself into positions of authority as though he already had inherited the farm.

Jesus would have made it clear that the father in the story represented the heavenly Father of whom he spoke so regularly. Those who heard the parable would have discussed it and mulled it over in their minds. A fresh understanding of the nature of God would have at least begun to formulate itself in their minds.

Myths in Scripture should never be discounted. They need to be explored in depth. A simple definition of a myth is that it is a story that bypasses historical truth to tell a greater story that can only be understood in mythical form. The Creation myth found in Genesis 1 is not an attempt to present a scientifically sound way of explaining the origin of the universe. Look at the overwhelming theme: the Creation is essentially good. This story was written during the time of the Babylonian Exile when the leadership was in Babylon and the remainder of Judah was essentially in captivity. The message of the essential goodness of Creation—including humanity—was particularly important at that time.

The parables or minimyths probably never had historical basis. Rather, they were tales Jesus developed to reveal greater truths about the nature of God and the human predicament.

A legend is quite different from a myth. Legends usually have some historical basis for their existence. Many years ago, I encountered a book that had been published within fifty years of George Washington's death. The author offered a story he had heard about George Washington accidentally scarring a prized fruit tree of his father. "When George's father inquired as to the author of the mischief" (I recall the phrase because it was so delightfully stated), George acknowledged that it was he. His father was so taken by the lad's honesty that he let him go without any punishment. Over the years, that vague account took a more elaborate form. The prized fruit tree became a cherry tree, and George's accidental scarring became an intentional chopping down of the tree. This is the typical way in which legends are created.

The purpose of many legends is to emphasize a certain quality in a person. This eventually becomes larger-than-life but still is believed by many. The story of Jesus calming the raging sea falls in the category of legend. I can only speculate about its origin, but I am certain that this tale serves no useful purpose. I doubt that anyone believes Jesus is God's Christ because of the story. Rather, I suspect that those who do believe this tale do so because they first believe Jesus is God's Christ.

Additionally, you should know that a form of fiction that was common to the ancients during times of adversity was called revelation. It allowed oppressed people to express themselves without putting themselves in danger for an act of treason. For some unknown reason, there is a large number of people who have organized their faith around two of these books of revelation or apocalypse: Daniel from the Jewish Bible and Revelation from the Christian Bible. Modern scholarship has clearly demonstrated that Daniel is a work of apocalyptic fiction. Jewish rabbis are bemused by those who believe it is actual historical fact. The book of Daniel is not included in their section on prophets but in that selection vaguely called Other Writings. Revelation has never been accepted by the Eastern Church, even if it is included in their canon. It simply has no value for them. How any scholar can relate its author to that of the Gospel and letters attributed to John is a mystery. He clearly identifies himself as John of Patmos and claims authority as a prophet. Had he been the apostle John, that would have been a much greater claim to authority. Aside from that, the theology is incompatible with the writings we attribute to the apostle John.

If you can accept these premises, this book might be for you. If you desire to enrich your faith with a fresh and valid understanding of the value of Scripture to your spiritual journey, then begin to read the pages carefully, thoughtfully, and reflectively. These brief essays will show you how to recognize false assumptions and contradictions. They will help you to recognize and accept the fact that the ancients were more concerned with wisdom than knowledge. They will help you to see and understand the people of Scripture and how the writers of Scripture were much as you and I. I hope they help you to understand that you and I follow in their footsteps and have the task and ability to be the people of Scriptures and to add to the story.

Drop the magic if you want to understand Scripture. There was no "magic era" when God behaved differently than God does today. Albert Einstein said it well: "God is a scientist—not a magician." There is no first-, second-, or third-century suggestion that Scripture was in any way dictated by God. It was not until the fourth century that Scripture even was declared to be *canon*. The term *canon* came from the word for *reed*—used as a yardstick in those times. In 2 Timothy 3:16, we read, "*All Scripture is inspired by God and profitable for teaching, for reproof, for correction, for training in righteousness.*" The writer obviously was referring to the Jewish Scriptures that had been accepted as canon prior to the writing of the letter. The term *inspired* means *God breathed*, not *God dictated* as so many uninformed self-designated scholars claim. The Scriptures were written by ordinary men who felt inspired to write them. They wrote from their humanness, their perspectives, their understandings of the world and society in which they lived—their human biases. As I mentioned earlier, the term *bible* means *library*. The Holy Bible—like any library—contains various types of books.

Some of the books in the Jewish Bible (Old Testament) obviously use more primary sources for their information. The book of Jasher is cited in Joshua 10:13 and 2 Samuel 1:18. The book of the War of the Lord is cited in Numbers 24: 14. The book of Songs is cited in 1 Kings 8:12–13. The Acts of Solomon is cited in 1 Kings 11:41. The writers readily tell their source of information. They do not claim to be eyewitnesses to the events they describe.

The books we call Chronicles (first and second) are obvious compilations. They cite many different sources for their information (e.g., Chronicles of the Kings of Israel and Judah, Sayings of Seers, Lament of Josiah, Nathan the Prophet, Vision of Isaiah, and Annals of King David). Scholars believe there were two primary writers for the books of Samuel, which explains the conflicting accounts we find there.

Scholars have identified four different major sources for the so-called *Books of Moses*. They are the J writer, so named because the name he uses for God is Jahweh (German), and he focuses upon Judah. The next is called E because the name he uses for God is Elohim, and he writes about Israel—which is often called Ephraim, for the oldest son of Joseph. Another is named P for the priestly writers who compiled the earlier writings and added their own traditions during the

Babylonian Exile. The D writer is considered to be the author of Deuteronomy, the scroll that was found in the temple during the reign of Josiah. The D writer also is considered the source for what scholars call the Deuteronomic theory of history. This is the underlying motif that those who worship God correctly will prosper and live long lives. The book of Job, incidentally, was a direct attack upon that theory. Still, that false theology continues to appear, appealing as it does, to the selfishness in human behavior. Today, it is called the prosperity theology.

SECTION 3

THEOLOGY

Why There Can Be No Single Creed or Theology

The first step in understanding how to do theology is to recognize and accept the fact that no single expression of the faith is suitable for all people, all cultures, all nations, and all times. My favorite professor, Dr. Albert Sundberg of Garrett Theological Seminary, began his basic introduction class by assigning three specific books on biblical interpretation and giving the students their choice of two others. Each book offered a different perspective on Scripture. He told the students to decide for themselves which perspective best fit their experience and understanding. Then he invited them to focus on that perspective with this understanding: "I do not care which perspective you decide upon, but I want you to be able to defend it intellectually."

He meant it, and this became one of the most liberating understanding and intellectually honest moments in my seminary career. Dr. Sundberg realized that we come from different backgrounds, have different personalities, and even different means for making decisions. Of course, no single statement of faith could resonate with every person.

John Wesley set forth four principles for biblical interpretation. We call them the Wesley Quadrilateral. Scripture, tradition, experience, and reason were the four factors that must be considered when one is attempting to translate the words of Scripture into intelligible, meaningful words for today's audience. Because I live in the post-Enlightenment era, I broaden the understanding of those terms in today's understandings of the nature of our universe.

Scripture still serves as a basis for understanding the movement of God in human history. However, Scripture should be read and understood with the best tools of biblical interpretation. The books of the Old Testament deal with many issues that have no spiritual value for us today. An old theme, of course, is the polemic of the land. If we read carefully and thoughtfully, we must note that the Abraham, Ishmael, Isaac tale is one of these polemics. Scripture acknowledges that Ishmael was the firstborn to Abraham and was therefore his rightful heir. His mother, however, was only a handmaiden, while Isaac's was a wife. That distinction is used to explain why Sarah had the right to drive her away from Abraham. With Jacob and Esau, we have a similar issue. Esau was the patriarch of the Edomites. The story of Esau and Jacob seems to say that Esau had the right to the land but that Jacob outsmarted and cheated Esau of his birthright. These and a few related incidents make for interesting storytelling, but they offer nothing of value to the spiritual pilgrim.

The many wars may suggest something of the power of the Jewish deity, YAWH, but they offer nothing for today's Christian.

The prophets are the worthier writings of the Jewish Bible for those seeking spiritual understanding from Scripture. These writers sensed beneath the surface and touched spiritual truths. Amos called for justice and mercy rather than futile sacrifice to the gods. Hosea sensed God's relentless love that we might call tough love today. Ezekiel may have had bizarre visions, but his messages were powerful expressions of truth and were essential for the exiles: God in a chariot could reach his people wherever they were; they were not abandoned. The valley of dry bones that would rise again gave hope. The vision of the restored temple was another vision of hope. The eighteenth chapter has been overlooked by those embracing the atonement theory. It refutes that idea with certainty. The Unknown Prophet of the Exile (Isaiah 39 to the ending) puts forth the idea of the suffering servant: the Messiah as a servant and not the Lord. It created the model that Jesus embodied.

The following are a few examples of human differences.

People can be defined as *tradition directed, other directed,* or *inner directed*. The first will feel secure and affirmed by following established tradition. The second finds security and affirmation through the feedback of others who are significant. The third relies on some inner compass or gyroscope to understand what is proper and true.

In his book *To Have or to Be,* Erich Fromm defines people as either security oriented or becoming oriented. The first will focus upon statements offering security. The second will focus upon statements calling for risk and change.

Jungian psychology will define people as either making decisions based upon logic or upon feelings and values. The significance is obvious.

Paul Tillich coined the terms *traditional* versus *conventional*. Those who are convention oriented believe that any change in form changes the content. Traditionalists believe that the form must be changed to fit the understandings of the existing culture. For them, any attempt to move a doctrine from one culture to another without altering its form is akin to trying to carry water from one location to another in a sieve. The form arrives but has no content. Tillich contends that these two types will not be able to understand each other. An example of a traditionalist was Jesus when he said, "You have heard it said . . . but I say to you." He found the content in the form and reshaped it for a present audience.

Within these parameters are cultural differences in values and life goals.

The task of the Christian preacher is to take a first-century Jewish event spoken in Aramaic, written in Greek and translate it into a meaningful message for the twenty-first century. Because of human limitations, this task is usually passed along to a few outstanding scholars who, unfortunately, often have their own private agendas and limitations.

Words mean different things to different people, depending upon their experience. Martin Luther, for example, had difficulty saying the Lord's Prayer because "our Father" was an unpleasant phrase for him. His relationship with his earthly father was not a pleasant one.

There are a multitude of other variables that make the possibility of uniformity of thought and belief astronomically difficult. Those sects or individuals that insist upon conformity are terribly naive and egocentric.

I place no value upon any of these conditions. They are just my way of acknowledging that there are too many differences in our backgrounds, perspectives, understanding, and personalities to allow a single creed or theology to fit everyone. Jesus said that we were known by our fruit. I have seen people with quite different interpretations of Scripture and understandings of God and Jesus who bear very good fruit. We take what we are given and make the best of it. That is the test of faithful discipleship. To quibble over semantics while people are starving, suffering, and dying—and are in need of our assistance—is antithetical to everything Jesus taught.

The proper place to begin this series of studies is with Scripture. The early Christians understood the role of these writings in their faith journeys. There were no early authoritative writings that served as guidelines for them. Books were handwritten, so there were few of them. As a consequence, the majority of the people were illiterate. There was no need to be able to read since few books were available. Information was transmitted orally. Seekers *heard* the stories. They were not written. The writings attributed to Paul, James, and John were copied and circulated. Although these writings were written to specific people, addressing specific issues, they served as guidelines for understanding the ethics of their new faith. Many writings claiming apostolic origin circulated during the early era. Many of them can be found in the Nag Hammadi Library, which was discovered in 1945.[1]

For various reasons, they were not included in the canonical collection we call the books of the New Testament. The word translated as *testament* also translates as *covenant*. The reasons the Jewish Bible was included with the Christian writings is a complex story. However, I will give a principal reason and let that suffice.

The early Christians perceived themselves as the true followers of the covenant. In their minds, they believed Jeremiah's claim that the old covenant had been broken by their disloyalty. He said the new covenant would be written on their hearts. When Ezra came to Jerusalem, he brought the new covenant written on scrolls. He also demanded the true Jews to be rid of their foreign wives and half-breed children. The Unknown Prophet of the Exile called for them to be a light to the nations. Ezra's demand ran contrary to that. It remained for Jesus and his followers to establish a new covenant that followed the stated form. Under Roman rule, Christians were not persecuted for their faith because the Romans perceived them as a branch of Judaism. It followed that they also would claim the Jewish Bible as their own.

---

[1] The Nag Hammadi Library was discovered in 1945. It contains writings that were considered heretical and were ordered destroyed. The range of thought is wide. Some are vastly different from that of the accepted canon. Others read much like the Gospel accounts. They reveal a style of thinking that for their readers were legitimate ways of understanding the mission of Jesus. They became the key to understanding the early movement called Gnosticism.

Early authorities were the apostles and their disciples. As they disappeared, those who had martyred themselves for the faith were venerated and viewed as spiritual authorities. Their writings were considered authoritative. When our present Scriptures were declared canonical in the late fourth century, they became the principal guidelines for the faithful. Documents from that time clearly reveal that they were considered authoritative writings—no more. Over time, however, the need for certainty crept into popular piety, and Scripture became more elevated in the minds of those seeking to be faithful. Later writings also reveal this. Scripture was treated with greater respect, elevated to the level of deity. It found its way to the central altars and was set before the cross. In time, the belief that these writings were in some way sacred drifted into popular thought. Rather than serving as a rule and guide as Paul declared Scripture to be, *they became the Word of God to be obeyed as law.*

The two major camps in Christianity today can be defined by their understanding of Scripture. Those we call Conservatives view Scripture as dictated by God, inerrant and demanding obedience. Those we call Liberals follow the thinking of Paul that Scripture serves as a rule and guide—no more.

With that brief background, I now will open the pages of Scripture to help you decide which of the two understandings of Scripture seems correct.

Two Beginnings

An observant reader of Scripture should notice that the book of Genesis contains two incompatible myths of Creation. Genesis 1 relates the later story, composed circa the sixth century BCE. It probably was written during—or shortly after—the Babylonian Exile. It was the Babylonians who created the seven-day week (*The Discoverers*, Daniel Boorstin). They believed the planet nearest to the Earth was the Sun (it's the largest, so it must be the nearest). The next closest was the moon. Therefore, they started the week with Sunday, followed by Moonday. The farthest was Saturn (Saturday). They believed that Saturn was an unlucky sign and therefore refrained from any venture on Saturday. The genius of the exiled priests was to take that idea and recast it into a day for reflection and rest. It has been said: "More than Israel kept the Sabbath, the Sabbath has kept Israel."

The priestly myth of Creation was written during a difficult time for the children of Abraham. The leadership was in exile. Those left behind were virtual captives ruled by a foreign power with a far different faith base. It is a magnificent myth affirming the essential goodness of God and the essential goodness of humanity. It was an uplifting message of hope and affirmation. It should be understood in that sense today. Any attempt to make it a scientific truth discredits the story and the interpreter. As noted earlier, even the order of the days of the week were based upon a false assumption. In this myth, God creates all existence in order, following a path that is akin to the present evolutionary unfolding of life on earth. The capstone is that God finally created man and woman and gave them dominion over all the earth—*"and saw that everything was good."*

The second Creation myth is the one used when the church speaks of the original sin. It tells a very primitive Creation myth. In this second myth, God creates man (humanity) "from the dust of the ground" (2:5), then decides man should not live alone. However, God seems to not get the idea at first. He creates animals that fail to resolve Adam's loneliness. Finally, he performs an interesting surgery and draws woman from Adam (2:21–22). He does not give them dominion over the earth but keeps them in a secure and peaceful garden. He had told Adam not to eat the fruit from the tree of knowledge, and apparently, Adam passed that information along to Eve (3:2). They do eat the fruit, however, so God casts them out of the garden and sentences them to a life of hard labor. To be certain they will remain outside the garden, God sets an angel to guard the entrance. Later, their son Cain slays Abel out of jealousy (4:8). God exiles Cain for this act. Then Cain and his wife have a son they name Enoch (4:15).

This should raise a question for any reader. If Adam and Eve were the first and only people created by God, where did Cain's wife come from? She obviously was not in Eden. If there were other humans created by God, why are we not told of them? Why were they not included in Eden? Had they sinned and been cast out? The tale has a gap in it that negates any historic validity. It is a myth, pure and simple, that is attempting to convey an idea that is best expressed as a story. Myths are not required to operate with logic. They are designed to convey a thought best expressed in story form. However, there is a great truth being told by that simple tale, perhaps one far more intuitively meaningful than the carefully crafted tale of the priests.

Most people relate to the sense of having fallen—from Eden or from innocence. A psychological explanation would be related to the development of the ego within the emerging child. Somewhere along age two, the ego develops to give a sense of self. As the ego develops, we increasingly feel ourselves separated from others, and we develop a greater sense of self and our boundaries. This development of a strong ego is absolutely essential to our development as a self-sufficient, autonomous human being. That process, however, generates what for most of us is the fall. As parents, we call this era in our children the terrible twos. We also often suffer the feelings of being abandoned or betrayed in some way. That either generates or adds to our sense of fall. These feelings are deep-seated and usually fall below the level of consciousness. However, they are present within us and affect our overall sense of self. Unfortunately, some people feel betrayed or abandoned before the sense of security has been developed. Their remembrance of Eden is dim. There may be a longing for a return to Eden, but it is vague, at best. Their dominant longing is for security. They build their lives upon a sense of basic mistrust rather than trust (*Stages of Development* by Eric Erickson). They are what Erich Fromm would call security-oriented people (*To Have or To Be by Erich Fromm*).

Some years ago, the Vatican ceased teaching that the Creation myths found in Genesis were historically true. The Enlightenment of the eighteenth century had freed humanity from superstitious beliefs with the development of the scientific method. The Roman Catholic Church recognizes these stories as the ones developed and passed along through the Judaic culture. Their interest is—as ours should be—in the ideas they impart. The idea of an original sin that was transmitted to all humanity at birth, however, is not one that was embraced by the Jewish faith. Read the Jewish Bible carefully, and you will not find a hint—apart from the Genesis story—of a doctrine of original sin. The prophet Ezekiel, in his eighteenth chapter (verses 1–10), actually denies its existence:

> *The word of the Lord came to me: "What do you people mean by quoting the proverb about the land of Israel: 'The fathers eat sour grapes, and the children's teeth are set on edge.' As surely as I live, declares the sovereign Lord you will no longer quote this proverb in Israel. For every living soul belongs to me, the father as well as the son—both alike being to me. The soul that sins is the soul that will die . . . Suppose there is a righteous man who does what is just and right . . . That man will surely live, declares the Sovereign Lord . . . Suppose he has a violent son who sheds blood or does those other (sinful) things . . . Will such a man live? He will not . . . But suppose this son has a son who sees all the sins his father commits, and though he sees them he does not do such things. . . . He will not die for his father's sins.*

Simply stated, there is no sin—original or otherwise—that is passed from generation to generation. You will find nothing in the books of the Old Testament that suggests otherwise.

The Day of Atonement was created for those sins that had been committed during the year. It had nothing to do with the Genesis account, or it would not be an annual event.

Read the Gospel accounts. Jesus never suggested that God was angry with humanity. He spoke of those who strayed from God. However, you will find Jesus's primary understanding of God is as a loving parent who readily forgives His children and welcomes those who have strayed from home—without any condition or reprimand. God also is spoken of as the good shepherd who went in search of a sheep who had strayed from the flock. Upon finding the lost sheep, the shepherd rejoiced. There was no anger in the shepherd—only joy. Jesus constantly told his listeners that God was their loving father. He never even suggested that God was angry, upset, or—in any way—alienated from them. How then did this fiction of *original sin* begin?

One unquestioned attribute about God is God's unconditional love. If one pauses to reflect upon the implication of the atonement, one must ask why a god of unconditional love required an atonement before being able to reconcile with humanity. The act of atonement obviously was a condition. Then one must press further to inquire why it is necessary to continually confess our sins before receiving communion. We either have been forgiven and accepted or not. Remember Ockham's razor as you wrestle with this. Complex, convoluted explanations serve no purpose here. Love cannot be both unconditional and dependent upon fulfilling a condition.

This whole train of thought is antithetical to Scripture. As I mentioned earlier, the eighteenth chapter of Ezekiel carefully spells that out. The sins of the fathers are not visited upon the children. Adam's sin had no effect upon his progeny according to Ezekiel. Further, the Jews saw themselves as the chosen people of God, destined to become a great nation. Nowhere will you find Jesus indiscriminately referring to all people as sinners. Rather, he calls them the light of the world and tells them to let their light shine upon humanity (Matthew 5:16). He also continually speaks of God as "your father" with never a hint of being alienated.

We humans tend to live with a sense of guilt. We have what Freud called a superego or what transactional analysis more meaningfully dubs as a critical parent,[2] who constantly tells us that we are not living up to some standard. We needlessly blame ourselves in many cases where we could not have affected the situation. Children often feel blame for their parents' divorce. Friends feel guilt for a suicide. For so many of us who are otherwise mentally healthy, we are our own worst critics and judges. Some families and societies are structured on the feelings of guilt and obligations. Incidentally, the more the family of origin used guilt as a means of control, the stronger the critical parent will be. The theologian who made the original sin a widespread belief was Saint Augustine. He had a brilliant mind but was troubled with a nagging sense of guilt. His confessions is a classic example of a person with an overactive critical parent. I believe this doctrine persists because it speaks to an unconscious or conscious

---

[2] Erikson, E. *Identity and the Life Cycle* (International University Press, Inc., 2016), 55–65

understanding of many. (*It also is a strong tool for manipulating people.*)

I have witnessed instances where the understanding that "Christ died for me" was helpful. The individuals were youths, poorly educated, and in trouble with the law. I imagine for those who wish or require simple answers and are troubled by feelings of guilt, this doctrine may grant relief. However, I do believe it would be more helpful to tell the troubled souls that Christ's death on the cross, calling out for forgiveness for his executioners, was a sign of God's great love and forgiveness for his human children.

The doctrine of original sin has never been accepted by any church council.

SECTION 4

Monotheism versus Henotheism

There is a significant difference between monotheists and henotheists. Monotheists believe there is only one deity. Henotheists assume there are many deities but that theirs is superior to all the others. There is strong evidence that Abraham and Moses were henotheists and not monotheists. This is not to disparage either or to minimize their contribution to our understanding of God. The original biblical languages call God by many names. El Shaddai, Elohim, and Yahweh are the most frequent when we read the typical translations. They are translated as God Almighty, Lord God, and God. The average reader unconsciously assumes the author has changed the terms in order to not be repetitious. This gives a false assumption that the author, or authors, write about the same deity. They do not. Each represents a different tribal god.

    The earliest understanding of deity was the belief that all life forms were endowed with some form of divine spirit that animated them. This eventually evolved into the belief in a veritable pantheon of deities, each with its specialty. We see this today as those deities evolved into the pantheon of Roman Catholic saints, who have their own specialties. The earliest supreme deity was Mother Earth. In his book *Sacred Eyes*, Robert Keck observes that this parallels our first need for a mother to nurture and protect us. He notes that settlements of that era reveal no trace of weapons of war or concern for defense. It was somewhere around 5000 BCE that the male warrior god began to appear on the human scene. At that time, traces of weapons of war and concern for defense began to appear in the settlements. An interim development was the pairing of a male and female deity of fertility.

Abraham's god was a tribal deity that Abraham believed had called him to a special mission. He obviously was not a warrior deity. Abraham was not an aggressive-conqueror type. He told his wife to lie in order to prevent a possibly violent confrontation. He even allowed her to be sexually used. He graciously welcomed strangers. Moses was a definite contrast. His deity inflicted pain and death on his enemies. His deity, Yahweh, conquered his enemies and took the land by warfare. Still, even Moses, in the Ten Commandments, ordered, "Thou shall have *no other gods* before me." This is a definite statement of henotheism. Do not try to rationalize this. A monotheist would have said not to worship *false* gods—not o*ther* gods.

Moses's contribution was in introducing a deity concerned with moral behavior. This deity of morality, however, was essentially lost to the descendants of Abraham until the sixth century BCE. This is where we will address the issue of accepting unfounded assumptions. A careful, thoughtful, and reflective student of Scripture would notice that there is only one mention of the Law of Moses from the time of the Exodus until well past the era of David and Solomon. That one mention is in 2 Kings 22:3–13. If one reads through to the end of chapter 23, it is obvious that Josiah's reform ended, perhaps with his death, but definitely by the time of Jehoiakim. The authors of the books of the Old Testament are silent about the nature of their deity, but there is no suggestion that it was the one who gave the Ten Commandments.

More important than that is the fact that a careful, reflective reading of the book of Exodus demonstrates that the story of the Exodus, as written, is not factually correct.

I want the reader to understand at this point that what I have written does not weaken my faith in Scripture. Rather, it enhances it, because my seminary training has taught me how to read Scripture to understand the underlying realities that gave rise to the words. This is the understanding I wish to impart to you. This was the biblical faith of those early seekers who sought to reach beyond the little tribal deities of their time.

These are some of the more significant (and obvious) reasons:

(1) There is no mention of such an exodus in the writings of the Egyptians. Their history revealed the failures as well as the successes, so there is no reason to suspect that the omission was intentional. Rather, a simple explanation is that it was not of great enough significance to warrant mentioning.

(2) Exodus 12:37–38 claims, "There were about six hundred thousand men on foot, besides women and children." If we were to assume that most of the adult males were married and that there were as many females as males, we could estimate that there were four hundred thousand families with an average of three children per family. That would add up to about two million six hundred thousand people. Exodus 12:31 reports that God told the Israelites to flee. "Take your flocks and herds, as you have said, and go." This presents a few issues:

(a) If they were given a decent distance between people for walking a long distance, a quarter of a mile-wide line would contain, at most, 260 people. Allow a yard between lines, and the line would extend for more than five miles. If you include the flocks and herds mentioned, you must add at least another two miles to that line. I have been in Ann Arbor and watched 100,000 people exit the stadium and head for home. With automobiles, traffic lights, and police guiding and controlling the flow for best efficiency, this process required hours to settle into something resembling order. Multiply this by 26 and add herds of animals, and you have, at best, chaos.

(b) In Exodus 14:10, we read that the Israelites looked up and saw the Egyptians approaching in their chariots. Even under the best of conditions, the Egyptians had to be within two miles to be seen by those at the rear of the column. Now, ask yourself how fast the chariots were traveling and how fast the Israelites—on foot with herds of animals—could travel. Does it begin to seem possible that more than two and a half million Israelites could walk across the Red Sea or even arrive at the Red Sea before the chariots would have caught them? Along that line, archeologists now are convinced that the sea crossed by Moses was the Reed Sea—not the Red Sea. The Reed Sea was shallow, and stiff winds could blow a pathway for the Israelites. Vowel sounds were not used in early Hebrew writings, so the misunderstanding is easy to understand.

(c) One look at the water from the rock, and we will move on: Exodus 17 relates the tale of Moses getting flowing water from a rock. You (hopefully) can see this coming, but I will continue. How much water would be required to quench the thirst of a person in a hot, arid climate? According to my research, the average person—on a hot, arid day—sweats a quart of water every hour. Now ask yourself how much time would be required to allow two and a half million people to sequentially receive a quart of water. If you generously allow only ten seconds per person (a practical impossibility) it would take seven hundred hours to give one quart to each person (forget the animals). That comes to just under an entire month (twenty-nine-plus days). Sorry, folks, but in my distorted mind, I envision two and a half million sets of dry bones that are not going to rise again.

The essential message of Exodus still remains even in the dramatic but historically inaccurate account. That message—for me at least—undergirds Romans 8:28 as it declares, "We know that in all things God works for the good with those who love God and are called according to his purpose." We do not know with certainty what transpired in the mind of Moses. We can assume he believed he was called by God to free the children of Israel who were held captive and to guide them into a morally grounded faith.

For the Jewish community, I believe their Good News is contained in the belief that "the God who brought you out of captivity and led you through the wilderness into the Promised Land can free you from whatever captivity would claim and bind you, guide you through your wilderness experience, and lead you into your promised land."

Do bear in mind that the actual books we call the Books of Moses, or the Pentateuch, actually were written during the Babylonian Exile in the sixth century BCE (before the Common Era). They were constructed out of earlier manuscripts, oral tradition, and the collective memories of those who wrote them. These were the ones we call the priestly writers. As priests, they had a high concern for the proper worship of the community. This is obvious to any discerning reader. God appears excessively concerned with the manner in which the people will worship him rather than the safety and care of the people themselves.

Now I would like to share my conjecture of what I believe actually occurred. In order to gain a fuller understanding of the events, you should read both Exodus and Numbers, seeing them as two different perspectives on the same story.

It was the tribe of Levites that was held in bondage in Egypt. They had Egyptian names. The members of the other tribes did not. During their travels, they encountered and joined with other wandering tribes, much as the early pioneers in our nation joined with other wagon trains in their journeys. This gave greater security and access to more resources. It is obvious that the tribes had greater loyalty to one another than to the entire group. I believe some of the tribes joined by default, arriving in the same area and being outsiders to the Canaanites who essentially controlled the rich fertile valley land. If you think in terms of a few hundred rather than two and a half million, it certainly explains those issues I mentioned. The Levites became the special religious leaders of the combined nation. The direct descendants of Aaron claimed exclusive religious leadership, but the remainder of the base group fought for some privilege as well. They also were related to Moses. The book of Leviticus is their offering to the religious rules. The claim of the descendants of Aaron is based upon their claim that he was Moses's spokesperson. However, if one reads Exodus with care, it should be clear that Moses is quite articulate and needs no spokesperson.

The tale of the golden calf in Exodus needs some clarification. The object in question was not a golden calf but the goddess Hathor depicted as a golden cow.

The Exodus stories say, "These are your gods, O Israel." I would observe the obvious: (1) *these* is a plural pronoun, and (2) *gods* is a plural noun. How people settled on thinking of "these gods" as a single golden calf escapes me. If you were to travel to the Cairo Museum today, you would see wooden figures shaped like a cow that show traces of once having been covered with a golden plate that penetrated the wood. The writer of the tale was careful in some respects. He had God tell the Israelites to steal gold from their neighbors in order to explain how they, as virtual slaves, had gold in the wilderness. (This, incidentally, does not speak well of God. I am sure one of the commandments forbade stealing.) However, he stuck close enough to historical fact to place two deities into the story. The other was the consort known as Ba'el. This was depicted by a wooden phallic symbol. Moses has the people burn the idol and then grind the ashes. This cannot be done with molten metal. This test by drinking the ashes of the crime is common among primitive people. The sense of guilt and accompanying fear of being punished appears to cause nausea and thus a violent reaction to drinking the ashes.

The book of Numbers tells the story differently. Moses is confronted with a direct rebellion of those who desired to return to Egypt, where they were fed and safe. Shortly after this confrontation, which led to the slaughter of many, Miriam, Moses's sister, fades from the narrative. Soon after that, Aaron fades and is replaced by Joshua. Then we learn that Moses will not be able to enter the Promised Land because of a minor infraction. That excuse, incidentally, is so lame as to be laughable. God had told Moses to command water to flow from a rock, but Moses struck the rock to cause the water flow. I have heard pious sermons based on this passage and have considered them to be absurd spouts of piety.

Whatever occurred during this era is a mystery, but we do know (at least the thoughtful Bible student knows) that the Law of Moses was essentially lost until the time of Josiah's reform. However, most readers simply assume the continuation of the Mosaic Law and the worship of YAWH. In doing so, they miss the message of Scripture and often sound foolish in their misinterpretations.

The ensuing era of the Judges was a time of pagan brutality. The story of Samson has no redeeming qualities at all. Samson was a bully and a whoremonger. There is no suggestion that he acted in any way for God's purpose. His accomplishment was in killing his people's enemies.

Jephthah, one of the judges, had vowed to slay the first person to greet him after he defeated the Ammonites. His daughter was the first one to exit the house, and he sacrificed her. Again, I have heard pious sermons on this, asserting the need to keep one's vows to God. Does anyone believe this is in keeping with the tradition of Abraham and the Law of Moses? Read Judges carefully, thoughtfully, and you will not find a trace of the Mosaic Law.

In 2 Samuel 12:1–10, when Nathan confronted David for his sin against Uriah, he made no mention of the Ten Commandments. David had coveted his neighbor's wife (10), committed adultery (7), and ordered the murder of Uriah (6), yet Nathan never stated that he had broken three of the commandments. Instead he told a story of a poor man who had nothing but a ewe lamb, which was taken by a rich man with an abundance of sheep.

Solomon's Temple, as described in 1 Kings 6:23–35 tells of carved cherubim, palm trees, and open flowers. This hardly speaks of a person who was aware of the Ten Commandments: "Thou shalt not make graven images" (2).

In Nehemiah 8–10, we read of Ezra reading the Law of Moses to the people in Jerusalem. Nehemiah 8:7 told of the men who "helped the people understand the law." It seems obvious that those who heard were unfamiliar with the law or they would not have needed help in understanding it. The law, along with the books we call the Books of Moses, were written in Babylon—probably by the faithful remnants of the followers of Moses, who followed those who wrote Deuteronomy and placed it in the temple during Josiah's reign.

The actual beginning of Judaism can be traced to the Babylonian Exile. The leaders in that exile were the priests and educated leaders. They undoubtedly realized the importance of maintaining their culture, lest the people become absorbed in the more sophisticated culture and the children of Abraham fade from memory as so many cultures before them had. This gave the faithful followers of the Mosaic tradition the opportunity to revive their understandings and become the law of the people. They designed the law as a barrier against exterior forces. I believe some of the priests became a bit too zealous in trying to attribute the religious dimension to the God who led them from Egypt. Also, they were a bit overzealous in defending the heirs of Aaron as priests.

If you read the books of the Old Testament (Jewish Bible) carefully, you will see that the first clear statement of monotheism aside from Exodus and Deuteronomy is expressed by the writer known either as 2 Isaiah or the Unknown Prophet of the Exile. His writings begin with chapter 40. Whereas the earlier references in Exodus and Deuteronomy make passing reference to monotheism, 2 Isaiah carefully builds the case: 44:6–8, 45:18–19, 46:5–7, 47:8, and 48:12–13. Scholars can only speculate on this writer. We know not why his writings were attached to the scroll of Isaiah, the prophet of the eighth century BCE. His writings obviously belong to the sixth century BCE. He is the writer who wrote the "suffering servant" passages found in Isaiah 53. It was he who introduced the idea of a messiah who would not be a warrior like King David but a servant who would give up his own life.

Ezra can be credited with bringing the law to Jerusalem and establishing Judaism there. I believe he missed a great opportunity, however. He ignored Jeremiah's statement that the law would be written on human hearts and not in stone. He also overlooked the Unknown Prophet's statement that in their return, the exiles were called not only to restore the house of Judah and remnants of Israel but "to become a light to the nations that my justice would be known to the ends of the earth." Instead, he established a law that demanded obedience to the letter of the law, and he cast out those who insisted upon retaining their foreign wives and half-breed children. As I pointed out earlier, because of these oversights, he created an opening for Jesus of Nazareth to claim to bring that promised new covenant written on the heart and proclaimed to all the nations.

SECTION 5

BIBLICAL ERRORS

A basic, foundational premise of fundamentalists is the absolute inerrancy of Scripture. They insist that every word—every account—is historically true and that there are no contradictions. If this is your belief and *you wish to retain it, stop reading and give (or throw) this book away. You will not like or accept what follows—even though it is indisputable.*

In the story of David slaying Goliath found in Samuel, the editor of the source material utilized to write this made a major error. He had Saul offering to loan his armor to David for his encounter with Goliath (17:31–41). He even inserted a passage that blended David caring for the family's sheep and bringing food for his brothers and with David serving as a musician for Saul (17:15). However, he totally undid this in 17:55–58 when he has Saul asking Abner, "Who is that young man?" (meaning David). And Abner responds, "I do not know." Saul then ordered, "Inquire who that young man is." So when David returned from killing Goliath, Saul asked him directly, "Whose son are you, young man?"

And David answers, "I am the son of your servant Jesse the Bethlehemite."

It is obvious to anyone who can reason that neither David nor Saul know the other. The tale of David being Saul's harpist is incompatible with this account.

There are other problems with this tale: (1) Archaeological evidence suggests that the Philistine helmets extended down to cover the nose. Goliath's forehead would have been well protected. (2) Second Samuel 21:19 states that Goliath was killed by Elhanan, one of David's mighty men. There is a tendency for leaders to be credited for actions committed not by them but by their subordinates. During WWII, it was common to read headlines that followed this pattern (e.g., "Patton defeats Rommel," "MacArthur retakes Philippines"). *Everyone understood what actually happened.* Still, those headlines would have been more accurate if they had added the word *troops* after a possessive *s*. There were not two Goliaths, or we would have read of it. Most likely, the account in Samuel is the accurate one, and the former is legend. Either way, there is a contradiction.

Just as neither this nor the two Creation tales in Genesis cannot both be true, I will point out the obvious contradictions and errors in these two Gospel accounts:

I mentioned Matthew's concern that Jesus be considered divine. Here are just a few of the changes Matthew makes to Mark's manuscript:

(1) In Mark's account of Jesus's baptism, the statement of sonship is *private*. "You are my son, the beloved"

(Mark 1:11). In Matthew 3:17, however, it is a *public* proclamation: "This is my son, the beloved."

(2) In Mark 1:12, the Spirit drove Jesus into the wilderness. In Matthew 4:1, the Spirit led Jesus into the wilderness. The Greek term translated as *drove* means to thrust, shove, or cast out. Matthew did not believe that could happen to Jesus. For him, the Spirit led Jesus into the wilderness.

(3) Mark 4:35–38 tells that Jesus's disciples "took him with them in the boat." Matthew 8:23–27 states, "When he got into the boat, his disciples followed him." This is not theologically important, except it continues Matthew's pattern of Jesus leading the way—never following. Another interesting change is that in Mark's account, Jesus is sleeping on a pillow. In Matthew's, his head is not on a pillow. One has to read back to before Jesus boarded the boat to understand this. Matthew was using material not found in Mark. He has Jesus saying, "The son of Man has nowhere to lay his head" (Matthew 8:20). When he continues (now using Mark), he notes the pillow and removes it from the account. Again, this has no theological significance (actually I think it is funny because my mind envisions Matthew quietly pulling the pillow from underneath Jesus's head). However, it does emphasize the care with which Matthew protects Jesus's image.

A more significant distinction is found in the telling of the Last Supper in the synoptic Gospels. Only Matthew includes the phrase "for the forgiveness of sins." None of the other accounts suggests that Jesus died for our sins. We have no first-, second-, or third-century manuscripts of the book we call Matthew. Many scholars believe that this was a later pious addition added by some well-meaning scribe who, as with the book of Mark, inserted a statement that reflected current understanding. Personally, I believe the church made a major mistake when they chose the passage from Matthew and ignored the earlier Mark and the witness of the earliest celebrations of the Eucharist as reported in the Didache and other sources. This acceptance of a doctrine of atonement transformed the table into an altar and the giving of thanks into an act of penance. Also, in recognizing the errors in Scripture is the fact that the Greek term for the bread used by Jesus at the Last Supper is *harton*, which means "leavened bread." *Azuma*—or unleavened bread—is the only bread that would be used at what often was referred to as the Feast of Unleavened Bread (Passover). There are innumerable examples of other contradictions if you read carefully.

Two Nativity Tales

First, let's clear the air on the genealogies. They are incompatible. The belief was that the promised Messiah would be a descendant of King David. Traditions rose to prove that. Matthew chose one, and Luke chose another. There have been attempts to reconcile them, but they fell short. If one stops to think of it, both genealogies are futile. They trace the lineage back through Joseph, who—according to the tradition—was not the biological father. He did not begat Jesus.

The Gospel of Mark makes no mention of the birth of Jesus. For Mark (who recorded Peter's memories of Jesus), the Good News began with his baptism at the Jordan at around age thirty. Scholarship has ascertained that the opening phrase of Mark, "Here begins the good news of Jesus Christ the Son of God," should omit "the Son of God" because it was a later addition. The earliest documents do not have that phrase. That phrase, incidentally, is grammatically incorrect and seems to be some scribe's misguided attempt to take the centurion's remark in Mark 15:39 to support a later belief in the divinity of Jesus. The Eastern Orthodox Church accepted Mark's version. Consequently, they celebrate Jesus's birth on January 6. This was originally a pagan water festival but was transformed into the holiday Epiphany at a later date.

It is accepted that both Matthew and Luke had a copy of Mark when they wrote their Gospel accounts. They follow Mark's outline precisely. The earliest record we have of Mark's validity is a statement by Papias, a second-century bishop of Hieropolis. He states that Mark recorded Peter's memories of Jesus's words and action *"in so far as he could recall, but not in chronological order."* Obviously then, Mark created the sequence that was so carefully followed by both Matthew and Luke, even to the point of making the same errors.

Sometime after the church began, some birth narratives began to circulate. Matthew accepted one, and Luke accepted another. The two are incompatible. Both cannot be historically true. I doubt that either was, yet each tells a tale that contains profound truth. As a consequence, I believe and embrace both every Advent season.

Let's look first at Matthew's Gospel. Matthew was a Jewish-oriented writer. We would be impoverished without his version. He acted as a teacher for his Jewish followers of Jesus. He organized the teachings of Jesus in wonderful fashion. We call his introduction the Sermon on the Mount. He began with the Beatitudes. There he sets the basic tone for his teaching. He contrasts Jesus's wisdom with the generally accepted wisdom of the world (i.e., "Blessed are the poor in spirit"). The remainder of his book elaborates on Jesus's nontraditional values.

At seminary, I learned how to identify a writer's nonstated premises and purposes. Once learned, it is rather easy to perceive the motives and conscious or unconscious convictions. Matthew had three that are quite obvious:

1. He believed Jesus fulfilled all the Jewish prophecies about the promised Messiah. A thoughtful reading of his work might cause one to believe that Jesus intentionally acted to fulfill those prophecies.
2. Matthew believed Jesus was divine (as opposed to Mark, who saw him as a Spirit-filled human). Because of this, he modifies some of Mark's statements to be consistent with this belief.
3. Matthew did not like the Pharisees. They were the good, law-abiding people of the time. They were the ones who paid their taxes, worshipped as prescribed on prescribed days, and were community leaders. However, Matthew probably hoped that with the destruction of the temple and the forced exile of the Jews, the people would embrace the faith offered

by the followers of Jesus. Instead, the Pharisees developed Rabbinical Judaism, and only a relatively few embraced the new faith. None of the other Gospel writers are as harsh on the Pharisees as Matthew. One would do well to be aware of these three biases.

With this in mind, Matthew was aware that prophecies of the Messiah said he must be born in Bethlehem but also must come out of Egypt. I do not even suggest that Matthew fabricated the story. Rather, I believe that from the various legends that were circulating, he selected the one that fit his understanding. The serious student must maintain an awareness that there were no readily available tools for verifying information at that time. Most of the world was illiterate; consequently, oral transmission of tales and traditions were the accepted means of disseminating information. We have seen how stories are altered in our time, and there is no reason to believe that there was some magical era when an entire population possessed perfect oral recall.

In Matthew 1:18–25, Mary has no angelic visit. Rather, Joseph is told by an angel that Mary was impregnated by the Holy Spirit, so he takes her home but has no marital relations with her. Matthew has the angel cite the prophecy of a messiah, found in Isaiah 7:14. There is no journey from Nazareth to Bethlehem. Magi journey from the east to pay homage to the newborn king. They ask Herod where they might find the baby, and his priests cite another prophecy. This one is from Micah 2: to tell he must be born in Bethlehem. Indeed, when the magi arrive, the family is living in a house. According to

2:9–10, the star they had been following stopped over the house in which Joseph, Mary, and the baby Jesus resided. This might have been thought possible in a first-century world. With our awareness of astronomy, however, this is unimaginable. Stars are far too distant to appear to be directly over any specific locale. The same star that appears to be directly over the head of someone standing in New York appears to be directly over the head of a person in California.

The holy family is warned in a dream to flee to Egypt to escape the coming slaughter of the innocents. When Herod realized that he had been duped by the magi, he ordered the deaths of all male babies under the age of two "in accordance with the time he learned from the magi" (2:15–16). By murdering the children, Herod fulfilled another prophecy: Jeremiah 31:15. This strongly suggests that the child was born more than a year previous to the arrival of the magi. That makes it quite unlikely that Joseph had journeyed to Bethlehem to enroll in the census.

Now let's take a look at Luke. His Greek is of good quality. He joined Paul on his second journey. At Troas, the narrative begins to speak of *we*. It is assumed that this is the point where Luke joins in the journey and no longer writes in the third-person plural. Because of his vocabulary, it was thought he might be schooled in medicine. However, there is no direct proof to support that speculation. We do not read of instances where he ministers to anyone's physical injuries or illnesses.

Luke had a monumental task in writing his version of the Gospel. He had to convince his readers that a man executed by Roman law and whose followers also were imprisoned or executed by Roman law was the person they should turn to as the agent of God who could give them eternal life. Note when you read Luke that he made a point out of finding no fault in Jesus and that the centurion found no fault in Paul. He also realized that the term *messiah* has no meaning for his readers. Additionally, the term *Son of God* was not unique. Many Roman emperors were considered *sons of God*. Plato had been given this designation also. He settled on the term *kurios*, which translates as *lord*. A lord had authority and deserved honor. In a polytheistic society, this was the best term available to him.

Luke's birth narrative told of the census ordered during the reign of Quirinius as governor of Syria. His use of this narrative told any reputable scholar that Luke was not schooled in thinking analytically as he read. The Romans were known as skilled administrators. Since there were no birth records kept during this era, it would have been absurdly foolish to have conducted a census in this manner. These are the most obvious reasons:

1. There would be no accountability. Since the Romans were considered to be unwanted intruders, nobody would assist them. Anyone who wished to avoid the census had merely to pack up and leave his residence. The Romans would have to assume the person was returning to the place of his birth. However, there would be no way to verify this.
2. It would have created uncontrollable chaos. Homes and businesses would be abandoned—ripe for looting.
3. Towns and villages would overflow with unexpected visitors who had no place to stay.

Aside from that, although the census was ordered, it was quickly abandoned because of the anger and resistance it generated. Galilee never had a census. It did not happen. Luke, of course, did not know this, so he simply told his narrative as he had received it, without thought for what it would have caused in confusion and waste.

Both narratives have value, however, if one delves beneath the surface. Every Advent and Christmas season, I embrace them and believe the stories beneath the stories.

Matthew said that this event, in one form or another, had to happen. He believed God has a habit of producing prophets, leaders, and reformers when there is a need for them. Joseph appeared when Israel and his children were in peril. Moses was called forth to free the captive children of Israel from Egypt. Amos spoke out when the corruption of Israel had become intolerable. "Come thou long-expected Jesus" says it well. In later days, Martin Luther, John Wesley, Abraham Lincoln, Gandhi, Harriet Tubman, Susan B. Anthony, Winston Churchill, and many, many others stepped forward in times of great need. The faith of Abraham and Moses had become a form of restrictive, joyless bondage. Matthew believed God would intervene.

Herod feared the newborn child, as despotic leaders continue to fear and repress expressions of truth. That dynamic continues today. Matthew's tale proclaims these truths.

Luke's narrative also proclaims a truth: there was no room for Jesus in the normal course of events. He was of humble origin and only recognized by the lowly and outcasts of society. Even today, it is the lowly congregations that are more apt to act in the manner of Jesus. In my experience, it is the inner-city congregations that actively minister to the poor and the outcast. "Infant holy, infant lowly for his bed a cattle stall."

Each Advent, I sing the words of the hymns and believe their message.

"The hopes and fears of all the years are met in thee tonight."
"Come, thou long-expect Jesus, born to set his people free."
"How silently, how silently, the wondrous gift is given. So, God imparts to human hearts the glories of his Heaven."

His birth needs to be celebrated—complete with myths, legends, and carols that speak truths more profound than the words tell.

The Last Supper

The synoptic Gospels present an entirely different picture of the Last Supper than the Gospel of John. Even the date differs.

Remember that none of the writers of the synoptic Gospels had seen Jesus in the flesh. Mark had traveled with his uncle, Simon Peter, for years and knew his stories. When Peter was crucified, Mark recorded the stories "in so far as he could remember" (said Papias, bishop of Hieropolis). Matthew and Luke obviously had a manuscript of Mark, for they follow his chronology precisely.

The synoptic Gospels claim that the Last Supper was the Passover meal. This presents two major problems:

1. The bread served at the meal is leavened bread. As mentioned earlier, there are two distinct terms for bread. One denotes leavened bread, and the other denotes unleavened bread. The terms are as distinct as *bread* and *crackers*. They are *harton* (leavened), which was served at the meal. This would not have been done at a Passover meal, which often was referred to as *ho azumon* (the unleavened bread). When I was younger, I was given an unleavened wafer at our communion services. Today, leavened bread is served. Interestingly, someone finally recognized or acknowledged that it was leavened bread that was served. Still, they hold fast to the tradition that it was the Passover meal. The symbolism was too good to dismiss, I suppose. Additionally, there is no mention of the food that would have been served at a Passover meal. Jesus was too much of an opportunist to have overlooked lamb as a symbol of sacrifice. Instead, he chose to use leavened bread as a symbol of his body.
2. "There was evening and there was morning: the first day" (Genesis 1:5). The Jewish day begins at sunset—not sunrise. Therefore, according to the synoptics, Jesus was crucified on Passover. This would not have been acceptable to the Jews. In John's account, Jesus must be removed from the cross before sunset because the coming day was the Sabbath. The Jews begged Pilate to have Jesus's legs broken and have him removed from the cross (John 19:31).

3. The early followers of Jesus celebrated the meal weekly—not annually. The Passover was an annual event. The food served was that which was served at the weekly kiddush. The kiddush was experienced weekly by the men of the community. They met on the eve of the Sabbath to prepare themselves for the holy day. They shared a simple repast of bread, cheese, olives, figs, wine, and an assortment of other light food. This meal was called the Eucharist (the giving of thanks). It was not perceived as a sacrifice for the first few centuries.

John's account says that the final meal was served prior to the Passover (John 13:1). There is no symbolism of bread and wine as Jesus's body and blood. Rather, Jesus washes his disciples' feet as a model that they, too, should serve as servants to others.

These diverse accounts cannot be reconciled. Those who claim the Bible is inerrant and infallible simply either have never read it or have not employed critical thinking while doing so.

SECTION 6

QUESTIONABLE DOCTRINES

I have claimed that the early theologians were basically philosophers. They were not biblical scholars. At seminary, I took a class in which each student was given the assignment of thoroughly reading an early theologian to see what Scriptures they used for their deliberations. We were shocked to see how rarely any of them referred to Scripture. They appeared to draw from the values and philosophy of their cultures in opposition to the witness of Scripture. As a result, some of their teaching—or doctrines—are either nonbiblical or actually contrary to the witness of Scripture. Some of these are minor in the manner they shape our faith. However, some are quite significant, and I believe they led us away from the original message and mission of Jesus Christ.

I will divide this section into two parts: the major and the minor questionable doctrines. I realize this will contain some thoughts that may upset you. Some of these are beloved doctrines we have believed throughout our lives. I ask you to consider the case I present for each teaching. Please do not discard them simply because they displease you. Jesus said, "If you continue in my way, you shall know the truth, and the truth will set you free." I do not claim that my offerings are the only truths, but I do sincerely believe they are well-grounded in Scripture, reason, experience, and our present understanding of Creation. I also believe they are liberating ideas that allow a person to live more fully and freely.

Section 6A: Questionable Major Doctrines

The Trinity: How and Why It Developed

"Holy, holy, holy . . . God in three persons. Blessed Trinity." Every Christian is familiar with this concept. For Christians, it is Gospel! The problem, however, is that it *is not Gospel*. The concept of the Trinity is, in fact, not only unsupported by the Gospel accounts, but *it is in contradiction to the witness of Scripture*.

"Not so!" you may want to shout. It is a doctrine that has been drilled into you since childhood. How could it be wrong?

If you will follow my explanation of the development of this doctrine carefully—thoughtfully—I will do my best to explain.

Perhaps I should first explain that my doctoral focus was on the first four hundred years of the church. Within that, my specialty was the development of the doctrine of the Trinity and Christology. I realized that Scripture did not support a Trinitarian understanding of deity. I also observed the varied concepts of Jesus Christ. I worked my way through labyrinths of documents to arrive at a theory that I could understand

and accept. The answer—or answers—are complex. First one must have some knowledge of the prevailing philosophy, or common understanding, of life. Hellenism is the name given to the philosophy of ancient Greece that extended from Socrates, Plato, and Aristotle to well into the Christian era. It also may be referred to as the Greco-Roman culture. Although Rome was the world empire, they were largely Hellenistic in thought. Any philosophy introduced into a society must adapt to the prevailing culture. The Hellenism of the first century had blended with Roman culture. It was different in many ways from the culture that shaped ancient Greece. Still, the fundamental principles prevailed. The Jews, dominated as they were by Rome, were strongly influenced by Hellenistic thought. The so-called Decapolis (ten cities), which the Romans had placed in Galilee, were Hellenistic. They had fewer religious demands and restrictions and spoke Greek as their primary language. The priestly caste of Sadducees adopted the Hellenistic style of life in order to remain in privileged relationship to the Roman leadership. Eventually, the law of the land was closer to the Roman law than that of Moses. The ultraconservative Pharisees struggled to maintain the Mosaic Law, for they recalled the statement of Jeremiah that told the people their defeat and exile was the penalty for breaking the Mosaic Law.

The moment the early Christianity moved into Roman culture, it began to change. The focus began to evolve from concern for the community and others to concern for self. The earliest refugees from fallen Jerusalem into Antioch selected the inner city as their residence in order to care for those they considered most needful. Over the years, however, the Roman Christians dominated the movement, and the focus upon the poor was lost.

One form of Greek philosophy was Stoicism, which stressed the natural law as a guiding force. Add to that the Roman emphasis upon civil law, and you understand how Roman Christianity developed into papal law.

It is Stoicism that was foundational in the thinking of the author of the Gospel of John. The concept of a divine *logos*—always badly translated as *word*—was introduced by John as a definition of the Son.

There were two Greek words that were translated as *word*. One quite literally meant the spoken or written word. The other (*logos*) denoted the underlying structure that gave substance to a word. (The philosophical structure of the early Greeks was quite different than ours. That idea has no meaning for us today.)

First Person: The Father

We will start with the doctrine of the Father. This should be relatively simple. It was the foundation for the other two persons.

Gods were thought of in anthropomorphic terms. They had physical bodies. The gods of Rome, Greece, Egypt, and the Norse were envisioned as being in human form. They may have been remote in heaven, Mount Olympus, or elsewhere, but they were physical. Worshippers often made images of them. In the more sophisticated philosophical schools, deity was considered to be totally transcendent—unknowable and unreachable by humans. The Father was the benevolent overseer and ultimate judge of humanity.

The Jewish deity of the Exodus dwelt with his people. He was present to them. The temple was even thought of as his dwelling place. This understanding simply was not available to Hellenistic thought. As a consequence, the Hellenists had no way of speaking about experiencing the divine in their lives. A remote, unknowable deity gives the religion a different texture than one who is present. There can be no sense of intimacy—no sense that the deity understands or is responsive to the worshipper. Prayers are cast into space. There is more the feeling of a judgmental spectator god than one who participates in the daily lives of believers.

At this point, I want to write about the notion that God is good. Many congregations have adopted a liturgy that proclaims, "God is good all the time, and all the time, God is good." I have watched this phenomenon develop over the years. Worshippers seem to enjoy it. I even hear it quoted outside of worship. Everyone nods in agreement and seems to relish the thought.

This thinking would have sounded strange to the prophet Amos. He asks, "Can evil befall a city unless the Lord has planned it?" (Amos 3:6). The radical monotheism of his time did not allow for a special deity in charge of evil. God was the Creator—the author—of everything. It was Persian duality that allowed an evil deity to cleanse the Jewish god of any taint of evil. The concept of a devil arose after the encounter with Persian culture. Apart from that, there is no hint in Scripture that "God is good all the time." In his masterful drama *J.B.* (in which Archibald MacLeish placed the book of Job in a modern setting), the character Nickles (Satan) states, "If God is good, he isn't God. And if God is God, he isn't good." By this, he refers to the deity that people believe has the ultimate control of the universe and can part the waters, calm the storm, or make the sun stop in the sky. Any cursory exploration of daily life denies the goodness of a deity who would allow the many destructive things that regularly happen.

The earthquakes and thousands of people are slain or injured. A flash flood drowns an entire family that has taken a minivacation. A child is born with a terrible illness that will cause weeks of suffering before it takes the child's life and leaves the parents devastated. The list is endless, but you get the idea. Do you believe any survivor of these—or any of hundreds of other disasters—can say that God is good all the time?

If you are going to embrace a religious faith, you need to select one in which the primary deity's nature corresponds with the realities of life. Otherwise, you will have one of those "feel-good faiths" that collapse in times of crisis. I have seen far too many good, church-attending Christians whose faith was built on wishes and not reality. In times of crisis, they find they have no faith at all. Everything they believed has been proven false.

My God is the Creator of an orderly but random universe. In this respect, I am a Deist. However, I have seen and experienced miracles of healing and what I might call divine intervention. Still, this has nothing to do with God being good all the time. I rest my faith on Romans 8:28: *"For we know that in all things God works for the good with those who love him and are called according to his purpose."*

Jesus tried to displace the notion of God as a judge who demanded reparation and punishment with that of a loving parent. The implications are radically different from what we came to believe. A loving parent wants her children to grow to live a worthy, satisfying life and to become independent. But the theology that prevails in our faith is focused upon the shortcomings of the children. We are essentially depraved and incapable of saving ourselves.

Archbishop Anselm of Canterbury was an eleventh-century bishop who essentially undid this work by Jesus with his doctrine of satisfaction atonement. His very rational approach to theology credited him with being the founder of Scholasticism, the dominant theology of the Middle Ages. He based his thinking on the feudal system of demanding satisfaction proportional to the injury endured. Completely ignoring the teachings of Jesus, he decided that the atonement had to include extreme suffering because of the insult to God caused by Adam's sin. Jesus did not only need to die; he had to suffer greatly for the atonement to be effective.

As theology drew more from secular culture and a literal interpretation of Scripture—and less from the spirit of Jesus—it became increasingly legalistic. Because of the statement found in John 3:5 about no one entering the kingdom except through the spirit and water, baptism was understood to be an essential part of salvation (although earlier, John himself proclaims that the one who is coming will baptize by spirit and not water). With this realization, a concern for the unbaptized child developed. Should an innocent child be condemned to eternal fire because of this? The church in its mercy decided that the unbaptized simply spent eternity is a neutral setting—in limbo. This was from the Latin word *limen,* which means *threshold.* A liminal is technically the space in a doorway that is in neither room. This only pacified the people for a short period of time. The realization that the child would forever be separated from the family became unbearable, so infant baptism became the order of the day. Also, a nurse was assigned to give emergency baptism if the child was in danger of dying. This practice, incidentally, continues in the present.

In 1972 while serving as an exchange minister in England, I learned I also was the backup (weekend) chaplain at a local hospital. I received a call on a Sunday morning, informing me I needed to administer a baptism to a stillborn child. I dashed off to the hospital and spoke with the mother, who was distraught for a variety of reasons. I put on a gown and my stole (the symbol of my office), took the lifeless body of the child in my arms, and administered baptism. The child did not need it. God did not require it, but the mother would anguish over the lack of that act endlessly. In far too many ways, the church has backed itself into legalistic thinking, which has hurt—not helped—humanity.

Following the logic of the culture, it was determined that there must be a group not ready for heaven but definitely not deserving of eternal punishment. As a logical consequence, the idea of purgatory developed. That was where a person would suffer enough to compensate from sins but have the chance for reprieve. This offered the opportunity to raise funds to support the church through the sale of indulgences. I thought that idea had died with the Reformation. However, in a trip to Rome in 1970, I was approached by a monk shaking a money box, obviously asking for a donation. I dropped in an American dollar, and he handed me a heavy paper card. When I examined it, I saw I had purchased an indulgence good for reducing a specified number of years in purgatory.

By the Middle Ages, I believe the church has wandered so far from its original purpose as to be unrecognizable by the founding fathers. The emphasis on Jesus as a sacrifice to atone for our sins diminished his role as a teacher and model. Fortunately, there always have been those congregations and priests who remained true to the teachings and spirit of Jesus. Unfortunately, these tended to be historically insignificant churches and or monasteries and nunneries.

Guilt and forgiveness had become the dominant themes of the faith. Confession had become a weekly requirement. Martin Luther used to agonize over the thought that he might have omitted some of his sins in his confession and therefore still bore their penalty. In his reformed liturgy, he omitted the prayer of confession, calling it a man-made instrument of the devil. However, he soon sneaked it back in, much like a relapsed drunk sneaking a bottle into his house. He had become addicted to guilt and confession.

The dominant theology of the Reformation was not Lutheranism but Calvinism, named for its founder: John Calvin. Calvinism emphasized human limitation. The doctrine of predestination emerged as part of this. Predestination is not to be confused with the theory of predeterminism, espoused by B. F. Skinner at a much later time. Predeterminism was based on the belief that since we are a bundle of complex chemicals and chemical reactions, all behavior is determined by that, and there is no such thing as freedom of the will. Predestinationism believed that our ultimate destination (heaven or hell) is determined at our conception and we humans cannot change that. Calvinism saw life as a burden, calling us to be faithful to God no matter the consequences. It avoided anything resembling frivolity. The Puritan ethic that resulted called for thriftiness and diligence, serving God through our work as well as the other facets of life. Since good Puritans avoided luxuries and were thrifty, they had a tendency to prosper financially. Eventually, the thought that those selected for eternal salvation would probably have some sign of that in their lives evolved into the American Dream. Clean-cut young men could come to America and become financially prosperous through diligence, clean living, and proper use of the money earned. The fictional character, Horatio Alger personified this belief in the many stories written about him. Eventually the financial success became more important as a goal than as a spiritual sign, and the American Dream became a dominant theme in the culture.

Calvinism remained the dominant theology in the culture, however, and influenced the entire society. The Blue Laws rose from Calvinism. Stores had to be closed on Sundays. The great evangelist, Jonathan Edwards, created a revival by traveling the country and preaching his famous sermon: "Sinners in the Hands of an Angry God." Fear and guilt were the chosen tools for enforcing desired behavior. Hellfire-and-damnation sermons were the order of the day. We all were sinners because of the sin of Adam. We were estranged from God, and it required Jesus Christ's death on a cross to atone for that sin and make us acceptable to God. The prayer of confession became an established portion of the liturgy of most Protestant congregations.

In the eighteenth century, John Wesley, an Anglican priest, had a heartwarming experience of the presence of God. He began a movement known as Methodism, which swept England and powerfully influenced American Protestantism. He denied the Calvin concept of predestination. He contended that humanity had some freedom of the will. He also emphasized what became known as the social gospel that called for the Christians to participate in creating a fair and just society.

By the end of the century, the churches seemed to have found more of a balance. The Blue Laws remained, and worshippers thought of themselves as sinners. But heaven became the goal of the saved, and most people thought of themselves as essentially among those saved. By the 1950s, however, we began to slip back into a more negative understanding of humanity. This focus drew deeply from the writings of Karl Barth. At the start of the last century, Barth was basically optimistic about humanity. A prevailing theme among Protestants was that we would bring in the Kingdom of God in our lifetime. However, the terrible destruction of World War I eroded that optimism. Humanity, left to its own devices, was corrupt and incapable of self-redemption. By the end of WWII, all optimism was lost. Calvinism—with its emphasis upon sin, guilt, and punishment—crept back into center stage, and neoorthodoxy emerged. It was the dominant theology being taught at most mainline seminaries. When I began to understand it and its implication on human development, I rejected it totally. My basic optimism would not allow me to accept it. I realized this was a reflection of my personal history. I never experienced feelings of being rejected or being unacceptable. My parents did not use guilt as a manipulative tool, nor was I discounted or told I was bad. I was encouraged to think for myself, to be independent, and to attain worthy goals.

Of course, I rejected neoorthodoxy. It ran contrary to my life experiences. Paul Tillich was my literary theological mentor. His sermon "You Are Accepted" affirmed my own belief, and he probed beneath the surface of ideas to reveal powerful principles and insights. It was Tillich who began speaking of God as the ground of being. This developed into a deeper and, I believe, more realistic understanding of that which we call God. It moves God from any category that resembles humanity and places God in a greater light that—with the mystery—renders God as more powerful, more magnificent than ever.

One theological statement I have heard since my childhood is that humanity's purpose is to praise and glorify God. Frankly, from the time I was mature enough to begin to reflect upon theology, I thought the idea was absurd. Further, it degraded God. If one is to flesh out how this idea developed, you would have to envision God, dwelling in some realm beyond time and space, saying to himself, "I don't feel good about myself. I need creatures who will praise and glorify me." My God does not have ego problems. I find that people who fish for compliments are rather unsure of themselves. They need others to prop up their egos in order to feel secure about their self-worth. My God, the God revealed by Jesus Christ, does not.

Second Person: The Son

There are a multitude of publications on this issue. How did a Jewish carpenter become divine? More specifically, how did this Jewish carpenter who was crucified as an enemy of the state become equal to the Father and eventually a part of the Godhead? Various factors played a role in this development. Ultimately, politics played a significant role. However, I will focus on what I believe were the two primary factors in the development: soteriology (the doctrine of salvation) and monotheism. Actually, the issue of soteriology was the driving factor. How could this carpenter of Nazareth bestow immortality on humans? The answer was made complex by Hellenistic thought. The issue of monotheism rose as a subsidiary issue.

To understand how this doctrine developed, I must remind you that what we now call Holy Scriptures had not attained that exalted title. There were many writings being circulated and used by the early Christians. It would require decades—even centuries—to pass before the church would set aside specific writings and declare them to be authoritative. Consequently, as I have noted with few exceptions, the early theologians were not biblical scholars but philosophers at best. They drew from the prevailing philosophies to reason their way through difficult understandings. Had they been guided by what we now call the books of the New Testament, they certainly would have arrived at different decisions. There are far too many statements there that suggest Jesus is less than God. However, in their attempt to equate Jesus with the Father, they utilized the concept of *logos* found in John.

As I mentioned earlier, what we now call Holy Scriptures had no official standing in the churches of the first, second, third, and most of the fourth centuries. Prior to their being declared canon by the Council of Hippo in 393 and the Council of Carthage in 397, the twenty-seven books of the New Testament were no more esteemed than dozens of other manuscripts that circulated at that time. Scribes felt they had the right—even the obligation—to correct them or update them as they believed proper.

A scribe did not have to understand Greek. He had only to prove he could copy it accurately. There are early documents that attest to that. The statement made by the centurion reads in Greek, *"Outos ho anthropos hious theou en."* Literally, this means "This [*outos*] the man [*ho anthropos*] a son [*hious*] of a god [*theou*] was [*en*]." Translators state this grammatically as "This man was a son of a god." The noun *anthropos* needed to be preceded by a *ho* (the definite article *the*) to become specific. In the same way, *hious* (son) and *theou* (of god) required a *ho* to become specific. With the specific articles, the phrase would have read, "This man was the son of the god." However, without the *ho*, the translation reads as "a son of a god." (Capitals were not employed to denote specifics.) In short, the scribe wrote it incorrectly to convey the thought he wished to express. In doing so, he demonstrated that the phrase was a later addition.

When Jesus was crucified, the centurion in charge made the comment *"Amen, outos hious theou en."* Surely this man was a son of a god. The centurion was a pagan who worshipped many gods. He could not have thought in terms of a single deity. Monotheism was beyond his experience. Frankly, I wish the translators had been honest in their work, but they understood that devout Christians wanted to read the popular version, that he was seen as *the* Son of God, so they made this erroneous translation. It is the opinion of many scholars that this pious, well-meaning scribe who inserted this clause in Mark merely desired to make the opening statement consistent with contemporary thought. He understood enough Greek to know the general meaning of the centurion's phrase even though he did not understand the grammatical rules. He therefore lifted that phrase and inserted it into the opening statement. The reader must remember throughout these essays that what we now call Holy Scriptures had no authority until the end of the fourth century. Prior to that, they were not treated as authoritative. Many early manuscripts contained additions that were identified and eliminated.

Follow me carefully and thoughtfully as I explain this.

Without that addition by the scribe setting the tone of divinity, the careful, thoughtful reader should notice that there is no mention of Jesus being divine or in any way equal to God the Father. Rather, his ministry begins when he is filled with the Holy Spirit. Then he sensed himself being thrust into the wilderness by that Spirit. (The Greek word *ekbalous* means "to cast out or thrust." It is not a gentle term. Certainly, the Holy Spirit could not thrust the divine Son of God into the wilderness—or anywhere.)

Mark's version that came from the memoirs of Simon Peter clearly perceived Jesus as a Spirit-filled human—*not* divine. Because the contemporary Christian has been conditioned to think of Jesus in terms of being God's Son, that assumption is unjustifiably carried over into the reading of Mark. *Christ* is the Greek for *messiah*. *Messiah* technically means "the anointed one." *King David was the first anointed one.* As with any folk hero, he became larger-than-life in the minds of his admirers. The people longed for his return to make things like they used to be. We see this with former pastors, presidents, and athletes. People look for someone who will replace their lost hero. So it was with the Jewish Messiah. The people believed he would drive out the Romans and restore Israel to the greatness they believe existed back in "the good old days." The Unknown Prophet of the Exile, whose writings begin in Isaiah 40, introduced a new, quite different concept of the Messiah (or Christ). He introduces the idea of the suffering servant who will sacrifice himself for others. The people of Jesus's time saw him as both models. There were those who hoped he would come with the sword and drive out the Romans, and there were those who saw him as the servant. Certainly, everything that Jesus said and did pointed toward the latter. With his resurrection, his followers saw him as the servant, and they adopted the servant attitude for themselves. The Gospel of Mark never viewed Jesus as more than a Spirit-filled man. Christ merely meant the anointed one of God.

Mark 3:21, 31–35 clearly state that neither Mary nor his brothers recognized him as special. Verse 3:21 clearly states they believed he was beside himself and went to bring him home from his ministry. Matthew 12:48 completely ignores the early portion and merely has them arrive at the house to speak to Jesus. If the birth narratives of Matthew and Luke had actually occurred, Mary would have been aware of the uniqueness of her son and would have supported—not interfered with—his ministry.

I have read absurd explanations of this in various commentaries. Most claim his family came to protect him from hostile forces and deny they thought he was in any way out of his mind. The Greek *exeste* (Mark 3:21) literally means "beside himself" (the best translation for that is "out of his mind"). Matthew omitted that portion of the tale in order to retain the sense of Jesus's divinity.

Mark's proclamation of Jesus as the Christ, by Simon Peter, is radically different from Matthew's. Since Mark is the author of Peter's memoirs, he should have an accurate remembrance of the moment. In Mark 8:27–30, Peter merely says, "You are the Messiah." Jesus immediately warns the twelve not to tell this to anyone.

In Matthew's account, however, Peter adds, "The Son of the living God." Then he has Jesus adding the words praising Peter and essentially anointing him as the head of the church (Matthew 16:16–18). There are two major problems with this anointing, however. The first is that James, the brother of Jesus, stepped in and assumed the leadership of the Jerusalem congregation (read Acts carefully). The second is with the claim that Peter was the first bishop of Rome. That belief was set forth by Tertullian more than a hundred years after Peter's death. He had no proof to support the statement, however. There are two issues here: (1) The early heads of the Rome congregation were called presiders—not bishops. (2) When Paul sends greetings to individual members of the Roman Church (chapter 16), he does not mention Simon Peter. He names many who are in that cluster of Christians but fails to acknowledge Peter as being among them. As noted, the belief that Peter was the first bishop arose much later, after Rome had obtained a high degree of recognition and prestige. The biblical witness does not support this claim. Actually, the two principal churches in the early church were Antioch and Alexandria. Rome became the referee (and tiebreaker) in their theological disputes and rose to prominence in the process.

The divinity was not an issue with the original Jewish People of the Way. Their anthropology was a simple one: *pneuma* (spirit or breath) combined with *soma* (body) to create a *psyche* (soul or living being). They believed in a physical resurrection (the only kind possible). The God who raised Jesus would raise the faithful ones. Problem solved. They did not question how this could be accomplished. Their expectation of a messiah was of a very human person anointed by God. Pay close attention to the writings of Mark, and you will see there is no clear theological explanation of Jesus's message and mission. His call to repent or transform the mind in order to enter the kingdom is never explained as either a clearly defined action or a consequence of obedience. The simplest explanation seems in keeping with the actions of the early followers of Jesus: develop a spirit of generosity, acceptance, reconciliation, and mercy to become part of a peaceful, productive, harmonious community wherein you will find peace, love, a sense of worthy purpose, and a vital relationship with God. The very Jewish letter of James expresses that quite well. If you want to understand the ethical foundation of the early church, you should read James. Unfortunately, centuries later, the noted theologian and reformer Martin Luther would call that letter an epistle of straw. He was so deeply mired in a concern for guilt and forgiveness that the original understanding seemed an obstacle to salvation.

As the Hellenistic world became the dominant Christian culture, a problem arose. Their anthropology was more complex: a body containing a soul and mind was enlivened by a spirit. The entire being was encased in *sarx* (flesh) that gave it its character. A fish, for example, was encased in a flesh that allowed it to live underwater. Birds had a flesh that allowed them to fly. In 1 Corinthians 15:44, Paul writes, "We are sown a physical body, we are raised a spiritual body." Just as the physical body allowed us to live in the physical world, our new spiritual body would equip us for living in the spiritual realm. Paul wrote this understanding of resurrection for the Hellenistic mind. A physical resurrection made no sense to them. It actually was inconceivable.

When a new religion enters a culture, it must adapt to the understandings and values of that culture in order to be understood and accepted. I noted earlier that many of the patristic theologians, although they were great thinkers, did not appear to be particularly familiar with the existing Scriptures. They rarely cited Scripture. Their focus was on explaining the theological issues relevant to their time—in terms familiar to their readers. They drew at least as much from their Greek philosophical thought as they did from Scripture.

As the Hellenistic theologians pondered the question of eternal life, they wrestled with the issue of how Christ could bestow eternal life on humans. A bishop of the late first century, Ignatius, provided the solution. He wrote a series of letters on his way to Rome to be martyred. In one of the letters, he referred to "the medicine of our immortality." Theologians grasped that phrase and assumed it referred to the Eucharist. To understand how this could help them explain the process by which Christ could bestow eternal life, you must first understand the underlying philosophical framework to explain the nature of things.

Matter was informed of its nature by its substance. That was its quality of being. Today, we would call that essence. However, for the people of that era, substance was a greater reality—a universal quality that actually informed matter of its nature. Each distinct item that existed had its particular substance. Each breed of animal shared a common substance. All breads had a common substance, as did wines. The theologians reasoned that when Christ held the cup and said, "This is my blood," he meant it literally—the same for the bread representing his body. Therefore, when a person takes the bread and the wine at the Eucharist, the underlying reality of those items (their substance) was transformed into the substance of Christ. Theologically, that is known as transubstantiation. (This is a current belief and part of the Roman Catholic liturgy.) If the worshippers actually followed the teachings of Jesus, the substance they ingested transformed their substance into that of Christ and would allow them to be resurrected as Christ was. This sounds strange to us today, but these people lived in the prescientific era and had a very different view of reality as a consequence. After they had resolved this problem, the theologians realized they had another issue: the common understanding of the culture was that anything that was created would eventually decay and die. Consequently, Jesus could only bestow immortality if he was uncreated.

This is when and why the almost-overlooked Gospel of John came to the forefront. I mentioned that John utilized the Stoic term Logos. It was his way of speaking about Jesus as *the Son*. For John, Jesus was the divine Logos incarnate. *Logos* is a difficult term to understand. I first learned it as *the world soul*. Over time, I began to grasp it as the aspect of divinity that was the will and nature of that which we call *God or the Father*. Read chapter 1 of John, and you will see this is the point being made: the two were actually one. If this is true, then the Logos is uncreated and therefore eternal. Incidentally, a careful reader would have noticed that entering the kingdom as a reward for obedience in the synoptic Gospels was replaced by John as attaining eternal life.

A careful reading of the Gospel of John also shows that whenever the Son (Jesus) is speaking, it actually is the divine Logos. This is why the statement "No one comes to the Father except through me" (John 14:6) is actually a tautological statement. (A tautological statement is true by its logical structure.) Since the divine Logos represents the will and nature of God, it logically follows that only those persons who become more Christlike will be on the path that draws them into a spiritual relationship with God. Christian fundamentalists overlook this and believe it means that one must literally be a follower of Jesus Christ. Actually, Jesus never suggests that but claims *"by your fruit you are known"* (Matthew 7:16, 20). Other New Testament Scriptures support this understanding (e.g., James 2:18, 3:12; Philippians 1:11; Luke 13:6–9).

Here is the summary:

1. The Father is uncreated, eternal.
2. The Son is the divine Logos, incarnate, also uncreated and eternal.
3. The Spirit *proceeded* from the Father (not *created* by the Father) and therefore also eternal.
4. The issue at stake became one of salvation (eternal life).
5. The substance of the Son was transubstantiated into the body of the believer at the time of the Eucharist.

This flies in the face of Scripture. The Gospel of Mark in its original form made no mention of Jesus being divine. He was Spirit filled.

In the Garden of Gethsemane, Jesus pleads with his father, saying, *"Nevertheless, your will; not mine"* (Mark 14:36).

On the cross, Jesus calls out, *"My God, my God, why have you forsaken me?"* and *"Into Thy hands I commend my spirit."* Those are not the words of a person who addresses an equal.

Even in John, Jesus says, *"The Father is greater than I"* (John 14:28). Also in John 10:29, Jesus says, *"My Father, who has given them to me, is more powerful than anyone else."*

Later, a deacon named Arius claimed that Scripture did not support the idea that the Father and the Son were identical in every detail. This controversy led to the formulation of the Nicene Creed, which asserted absolute equality.

Unfortunately, the acceptance of a false premise caused the council to ignore Scripture in order to allow eternal life. This moved Jesus from an example for humanity to being a sacrifice that saved a helpless humanity.

The Third Person: Holy Spirit

We now explore the concept of the Holy Spirit as part of the Trinity. Even as we prepare to do that, I am compelled to tell you of a statement made by the famous medieval theologian Thomas Aquinas after an exhaustive study of the Holy Spirit: *"The Holy Spirit remains a holy mystery."* Scripture only confuses the subject. It does not clarify it. This serves as a warning to you that the unraveling of this mystery will be contorted, is sometimes tedious, and must be followed carefully, thoughtfully, and reflectively.

The only time Jesus is reported as describing the nature of God is found in John 4:14: *"God is spirit, and they that worship Him must worship Him in spirit and in truth."* If we look at contemporary science to further pursue this, we are aware that prior to the big bang, there was neither time nor space. Therefore, whatever force created this physical universe must necessarily be without physical substance. That can be described as either *energy* or *spirit*. There is no other reasonable option.

The idea of a spirit apart from the Father is a result of the Hellenistic influence. God, for the Greek philosophers, was completely transcendent, unknowable, and inaccessible. This is a far cry from the God in Exodus, who dwelt with his people. It is, however, the result of a gradual transition from traditional Jewish thought to Hellenism. Cultures evolve slowly, and people usually adapt with little or no awareness of the changes (yes, old-timers may complain, but the younger generations discount them as being out-of-date and adapt to the new). Since it was inconceivable that humanity could directly experience God, the term *spirit* became a useful tool for speaking of the experience of deity in one's life. (We still do that today, saying "spirit filled" when speaking of those deeply in touch with deity). Another development of this belief in a transcendent deity was the development of angels. We shall examine that later.

Read the book of Acts carefully, and you will note that new converts were baptized in the name of Jesus, not the Trinity. "And Peter said to them, 'Repent and be baptized, every one of you, in the name of Jesus Christ for the forgiveness of sins, and you will receive the Holy Spirit'" (Acts 2:38). In Acts 19, we read of Paul asking the new converts at Ephesus if they had received the Holy Spirit. They replied that they had never heard of the Holy Spirit. So Paul asks what baptism they did receive, and they responded that it was the baptism of John. He informed them that John's baptism was for repentance but that they needed to believe in Jesus. Acts 19:4 records: *"On hearing that, they were baptized in the name of Jesus."* They then received the Holy Spirit. However, they were not baptized in the name of the Holy Spirit.

It should be obvious that neither Peter nor Paul used a Trinitarian formula for baptism. The wonderful story we call the Great Commission found in Matthew 28:18–20 is a later addition. It conveys the proper spirit of Jesus sending his disciples forth, but its language is anachronistic. The Trinitarian formula was a later development.

Let's look at the Spirit from another angle. A careful reading of Scripture reveals a few inconsistencies on the subject, but others offer a clearer, more useful understanding.

First the inconsistencies: It is understood that the Spirit is the source of power for disciples. It is at Pentecost when they are filled with the Holy Spirit that they are empowered to go forth, preach with power, and heal. At least that is the common understanding. This raises some questions, however. Luke 10 tells of Jesus commissioning seventy-two disciples to go out as short-term missionaries. They return, telling that, "Even the demons submit to us in your name" (Luke 10: 17). Jesus only *commissioned* the seventy. There is no suggestion of their receiving the power of the Holy Spirit. What then was the source of the power by which they were able to cast out demons? As mentioned previously, new disciples after receiving the baptism of Jesus also received the Holy Spirit. If this is true, we must assume that the original disciples must also have received the Holy Spirit. Yet scriptural accounts not only do not verify that but—as in the telling of Pentecost—seem to contradict that.

Mark 9:14–29 tells of the disciples' failure to cast a demon from a young boy. Jesus reacts by saying, "You unbelieving generation. How long will I stay with you? How long shall I put up with you?" Later, when the disciples ask why they could not cast out the demon, Jesus answers, "This kind can come out only by prayer." The careful reader should be aware that here is no mention of Jesus praying prior to casting out the demon. Yet there is the suggestion that the disciples would have been able to cast out the demon through prayer. Mark 1:35 tells of Jesus rising in the morning and going to a place to pray privately. His prayer life was the foundation of his ministry. In the quietness of the morning, Jesus communed with God. Here he found courage and power for the day's journey. He may have been filled with the Holy Spirit, but it was in the time of prayer that he drew most fully from the power of the spirit. He suggests that the others—though not having received a postresurrection baptism of the Spirit—could have been empowered to subdue demons through the power of prayer.

So I ask you, readers, is the Holy Spirit a gift we receive at baptism, or is it later bestowed upon either the faithful or randomly? Scripture suggests both, yet both cannot be true. Perhaps the Spirit is not bestowed at all?

The early followers of Jesus did not have the tools of contemporary science or psychology. The understanding of life had to be explained in other terms that may sound naive or primitive to us. In no way do I intend to discount or demean their explanations. However, I believe I can clarify the apparent contradictions and inconsistencies by employing those tools.

Today, we have no problem about speaking about experiencing the presence of God in our lives. We have moved beyond Hellenistic philosophy and incorporated such biblical statements as Paul's *"For in Him we live and move and have our being"* (Acts 17:28).

We hear people speak of "God within me" as a matter of course. Not only do we no longer think of God as totally transcendent, unknowable, and unattainable, but we think of God as residing *within* us. If the New Testament writers had been able to think in those terms, they would have understood and explained those events quite differently. We do them a disservice when we insist upon using their categories and dismissing our own.

I would propose that within each person is a spark of divinity that becomes displaced and ignored as we develop our own ego, complete with ego boundaries. We ignore our spiritual dimension and focus primarily—and/or completely—on our physical lives. Our ego-centered self adopts the values of society and lives a life of inner loneliness, lost dreams, and sense of meaninglessness. As with an addict who finally must admit some need, many listeners will hear the message of God's love and not respond. However, those who are seeking more may find the message of Jesus Christ resonating within them.

Let me try this analogy: A fine piece of crystal may sit on a table for years—totally inert. Then, one day, a musician passes by, playing an instrument, and strikes a note that is harmonically in tune with the crystal. The crystal begins to vibrate and even reproduce the sound made by the musical instrument. For me, this is consistent with the recorded events of newly baptized Christians receiving the spirit after they hear the preaching about Jesus. They resonate to the message, and the latent spirit within them becomes alive and active. To me, this also explains why those seventy-two disciples who had been with Jesus for a length of time were able to perform the exorcisms and healings they did. They had gradually begun to get in tune with Jesus and his message. Therefore, they were more spiritually alive.

I will try to explain the Pentecost phenomenon by comparing it to the beginning of the Methodist movement in eighteenth-century England. John Wesley organized the early converts into classes that met regularly for study and prayer. They met for months with no noticeable changes occurring in any of the groups. Then in a very short time, various groups began to break out with new energy and excitement. I compare it with corn kernels sitting on a hot stove for a period of time. If you have ever popped corn, you know that nothing happens for a while. Then you hear a pop and then another pop. Suddenly, you hear popping sounds that resemble a string of firecrackers: *pop, pop, pop, pop*. That seems to be what happened in England, and the Methodist movement swept across England like wildfire.

We can only speculate on how the twelve spent their time prior to the Pentecost event. If the event of Pentecost is to be believed, then we must assume the twelve had, in some way, prepared themselves for it.

However, in a conflicting account (John 20:19–23), Jesus appears to ten of the twelve in a closed room and breathes the Holy Spirit into them. For me, this account has less credibility. I will have to open a large parenthesis to explain.

The disciple, Thomas, is only mentioned in the Gospel of John. I believe these are later additions for these reasons: the Gospel of Thomas was considered to be a Gnostic writing. Some early church fathers were extremely critical of Gnosticism. Perhaps the strongest critic was Irenaeus, the bishop of Lyon. His work *Against Heresies* was all we knew about Gnosticism until the discovery of the Nag Hammadi Library in upper Egypt in 1945. There is a letter from Irenaeus to the bishop of Rome in which he complains that the Gnostics do not inform him of their meetings (as bishop, he should be invited to preside). The Gnostics did not recognize designated authority. Rather, they responded to and respected "inner authority."

When Thomas is introduced in John 11:16, he says, "Let us also go (to Jerusalem) that we may die with him." This sounds courageous, but Thomas later flees with the other disciples when Jesus is arrested. The implication is that Thomas cannot be trusted.

In John 14:4–6, when Jesus tells his followers that he must leave them and says, "And you know the way to where I am going." Thomas says, "Lord, we do not know where you are going. How can we know the way?" Since the early followers of Jesus called themselves the People of the Way, the implication should be obvious.

When Jesus breathes the Holy Spirit into the disciples in John 20, Thomas is not present. The implication, of course, is that Thomas did not receive the Holy Spirit.

We all know the story of doubting Thomas. That, of course, adds to discrediting Thomas as a spiritual leader. (In the late nineteenth century, explorers discovered churches that Thomas had founded in India—as tradition claims.) That strongly suggests that John's attempt to discount his faith was not solidly grounded.

John also is the only Gospel account to call Judas a thief (John 12:6). John has understandable anger toward Judas but seems unaware of the implications of his statement. There can only be two explanations of why Jesus would allow a thief to be custodian of the group's finances: (1) He did not know Judas was a thief. (2) He knew and allowed it. Neither of these choices speaks well for Jesus. I believe whoever wrote this allowed his emotions to cloud his memory. There are no first-or second-century documents to give clear information as to what was originally written and what was added later.

We have to rely on the tone and consistency of the statement plus common sense to guide us in this endeavor. Every writer has a perspective or bias. When we can identify that, it helps us to understand the writing and writer more clearly.

Now, back to the Holy Spirit. The Swiss psychiatrist Carl Jung believes that each of us possesses two natures: conscious and unconscious (subconscious). Our conscious nature is contained in what we call the ego. It is the aspect of our mind that establishes boundaries and the sense of self. Jung calls it self (lowercased *s*). He believes the unconscious also has an aspect of being that he calls Self (capital *S*), or *imago Dei* (image of God). The more spiritually mature an individual becomes, the more aware and in touch with the inner Self that person is. Jung believed that the movement of life should be: first, to become aware of all of the aspects of our conscious self and then to become fully aware of the unconscious Self and allow that Self to displace our ego. It is the scriptural idea of *being born again or anew*.

If we understand the Creation story in Genesis 1 as a myth, then we understand that it claims we humans are made in the image of God. Since God is spirit, we must be in the spiritual image of God or Jung's imago Dei.

Genesis 1, which speaks of the Spirit of God, was written in Babylon during the exile. The culture was Hellenistic at the time.

Many people today, because of the influence of the Trinitarian doctrine, refer to the awareness of the Spirit within them as the Spirit of Jesus. That is the way they have been conditioned to think. I refer to that experience of spirit as the presence of God within me. The precise term is irrelevant. What is significant is the fact that in today's society, we are capable of experiencing the presence of the divine in our lives.

When Mark records Jesus's baptism, he reports a very private and personal experience. Only Jesus hears a voice claiming him as His son. Only he sees the Spirit descending upon him as a dove (Mark 1:10–11). The image usually shown of the dove does not do the scene justice. The image depicted looks like a bird in full flight. Have you ever observed a dove landing? It settles and hovers for a moment, then gently flutters to the ground, engulfing any object beneath it. Jesus sensed the Spirit of God descending and enveloping him. Possibly, for Jesus, the vision at baptism was his spiritual awakening. There is no hint that, prior to his baptism, Jesus was special in any way. Luke 4:16–30 tells of him being rejected at Nazareth when the people realized he was just Joseph's son—and no one special.

Mark 1:1 reads, "Here begins the good news of Jesus Christ." According to Peter's memoirs, the baptism was the beginning of Jesus as God's Christ. There was not a hint of divinity prior to that time. Not until Jesus sensed himself filled with God's spirit and claimed as his son did he appear to be more than an ordinary human being.

Summation: the Holy Spirit truly is a holy mystery. The biblical witness is contradictory to any consistent definition. There also is no scriptural support for a doctrine of the Trinity. Since Jesus's only definition of God was expressed in the Gospel of John, "God is Spirit," it seems that the Holy Spirit is just another way of speaking of the experience of God. God the Father as the creative, sustaining force of the universe stands alone as deity. This deity is so far beyond human comprehension that we need someone more understandable to even begin to grasp His will for humanity. I think of Jesus as personifying all the positive traits of deity we humans are capable of understanding.

Atonement

Good parents want to raise children who have a good self-image, are competent, and are capable of being independent. They do not wish to raise children who feel unworthy, are incompetent, and will forever be dependent upon their parents. Why then do we Christians believe our heavenly Father wishes to do the latter? The doctrine that we are essentially sinners incapable of saving ourselves does precisely that. I know dear people who are loving and generous of spirit who live with a constant sense of unworthiness simply because that is what their Christian faith taught them to believe.

This belief flies in the face of New Testament teaching to the contrary. Jesus never called the people to whom he spoke sinners. He called them the light of the world" (Matthew 5:14). He spoke to them of their *heavenly Father*. The obvious implication of that was that we humans are *children of God*. That is our nature. We are not sinners but *children of the living God*. Also, Jesus never spoke of us as being alienated from God, nor did he ever even suggest that God was angry with us because an ancestor disobeyed him. His parable of the prodigal son depicted God as a loving parent who only longed for his wayward son. When the son returned, the father gave no recriminations or demanded any restitutions. He embraced the son and celebrated. To this, I would add that anyone who reads the eighteenth chapter of Ezekiel should understand that God is not concerned with who we once were but who we are now. Ezekiel clearly states that guilt and sin cannot be inherited. Jesus amplified this in many of his parables (Matthew 20:1–16).

To step outside of Scripture, I would add that the Jewish faith does not have a doctrine of original sin. This is purely a Christian doctrine. It seems unlikely that Jesus would have died to redeem us from something he did not know existed. I would add that it seems a contradiction of the atonement theory that at every communion service, United Methodists (and many others) must first confess their sins and receive forgiveness. What sin did Jesus die for that reconciled us to God if we still are sinners and must constantly confess those sins?

I believe this doctrine developed to solve a problem based upon a false assumption. That false assumption was that God operated on the same principles as we humans, and he would require some recompense for our supposed disobedience. The Gospels do make clear the reason Jesus died upon the cross. Matthew has a throwaway line about for the forgiveness of sins in the earliest copy we have of his account of the Last Supper. Since that differs from Mark, from whom he copied, and also from Luke, who used Mark as his outline, we cannot be certain that this is not a later addition. At this point, any current theologian schooled in biblical interpretation would employ Ockham's razor and use the simplest, most direct solution. Jesus died on the cross then rose from the dead. His death and resurrection demonstrated that human life does not come to an end when the body dies. We are in this for the long haul, so we should live without undue fear of death and prepare ourselves for some future existence. Jesus's life served as the model for what we should strive to become.

Summation: I believe the doctrine of atonement *that was never stated as* doctrine by any council is an unnecessary; it is destructive teaching and should be abandoned.

This leads us naturally to the doctrine of salvation.

Salvation

When people ask me if I have been saved, I have one of three stock responses:

1. My usual response is "I've been saved and lost so many times I am not sure where I am now."
2. "Yes, on a hill outside of Jerusalem, two thousand years ago." (I reserve this for the pious type.)
3. "I do not use that term. My God is not one from whom I need to be saved." (This one is for those I believe are willing to discuss the issue.)

Study the teachings of Jesus, and you see that our personal salvation does not seem to be an issue with him. He did suggest that people may stray away or consciously turn away from God and become lost. However, he otherwise seemed to assume that everyone was included in the family and fellowship of God. When the emphasis was put on personal salvation, it dramatically changed the tone of the church. Prior to that, the emphasis was on service to others, particularly those in need. They held all things in common (yes, socialism). Even the poorest among them was entitled to equal shares when they became part of the community. They were community centered. The message was simple. Jesus wrapped it up in what we call the Golden Rule, "Whatever you would have people do to you, do to them," and in his two great commandments: *"Love the Lord your God with all your heart, soul, mind, and strength, and love your neighbor as yourself."* Live the good life as taught and modeled by Jesus, and do not worry about what lies beyond this earthly life. God is the god of the living, and God will provide.

When the church moved to a quest for personal salvation, the members became more self-oriented, self-concerned. Originally, people were called to live their spiritual lives more fully. Jesus called this being a part of the Kingdom of God.

The Eastern culture was built on Platonic thought. As a consequence, they never developed a doctrine of atonement. Rather than believing Christ died to atone for human sin, the Eastern Church proclaimed, "The divine became human that the human might become divine." This is a radically different interpretation. A school of biblical interpretation developed in Alexandria. Unlike their Western counterparts, their theologians were biblical scholars. As we survey their history, we note that the leaders of the church never tried the role of political leaders. Also—and far more significant—the church did not go through a period of reformation, breaking down into hundreds of sects, as with Protestantism.

Section 6B: Minor Questionable Doctrines

These doctrines or common beliefs passed along by the church do not have the impact upon the underlying message and mission of the church. In my opinion, they merely distort our expectations.

Heaven and Hell

The thought of residing in eternal bliss is terrifying to me. I would be bored out of my skull. I simply cannot reconcile the God of this enormous, complex universe with the idea of humans receiving an eternal consignment either to a place of bliss or a place of punishment depending upon how they had behaved during their brief stint on earth. My mind envisions some kind of Rube Goldberg contraption in which an extraordinarily complex machine moves through a lengthy process to produce an extremely simple result, such as turning off a light. Fourteen billion years in the making... for what? Free harp lessons? The opportunity to sing in a heavenly choir? A guaranteed early tee time? I believe our Creator has greater plans for us and that we have not begun to arrive at the state of maturity He desires. Where we go from beyond this earthly life is beyond us. However, I am convinced there is more—much more. We take who we are and move on to another stage. As we move through this earthly life, we should be aware that there is more to come. This will require that we become all that we can become to fulfill our divine nature during this lifetime.

This imperfect earth is a wonderful classroom for spiritual growth. We have to learn how to build and maintain relationships. We continuously encounter little obstacles and frustrations that cause us to develop patience and reasoning ability. Losses teach us empathy and sympathy. As we learn to accept responsibility for our lives, we develop wisdom. Essentially, the imperfections help us to mature and outgrow childish ways. A place of eternal bliss could only cause spiritual stagnation.

Many of us have observed what happens with those who lived specially privileged lives. They are bored and boring. Life has to be filled with what I call distractions. There are those wealthy families, of course, that raise their children with a sense of responsibility for others—to use their wealth and privilege to help others with greater needs. However, the general path is the first one mentioned.

There are various models for what occurs after our last earthly breath. What I see as the common denominator of these different possibilities is that the consequence of living an egocentric life are unpleasant. This may range from bad karma for the next journey, to eternal separation from God, to nonexistence as a failed possibility.

Angels

I promised to make a statement about angels, so here it is: I have not been able to relate to the idea of winged heavenly beings flitting about, helping humans in time of need. I wrote about this in my first book and will give an overview of the evolution of my thinking in that regard. In the city of Ravenna, which once served as the capital of the western Roman Empire, there is a martyrium that has a mosaic of Abraham entertaining angels while unaware of who they were. I noticed they had no wings. By contrast, the Christian basilicas had mosaics depicting winged angels. This roused my curiosity, and I continued to watch for depictions of angels.

The city of Ostia Antica is about twenty miles outside of Rome and is far more interesting than Pompey. Pompey was a rather ordinary city that had the misfortune of being buried by volcanic ash. Ostia Antica was the port city of Rome. Claudius had it transformed into a resort as a gift to Nero. Their misfortune was in supporting Maxentius in his battle with Constantine. Constantine, of course, was the victor. In retaliation for their disloyalty, Constantine constructed a rival port city for Rome and transferred all government contracts to that city. Ostia eventually could not afford to maintain the river. The river became clogged with sand that overran the land and buried it.

In the 1930s, Benito Mussolini, the new dictator of Italy began excavations of the city as part of his plan to recapture the glory of Rome. World War II interrupted the operation, however. It was not until the early 1960s that the excavations were resumed. My professor worked on a dig there one summer and told us it was worth seeing. A few years later, I was asked to lead a study tour for college students. When we arrived at Rome, I placed a visit there on top of my off-day list.

Visitors can step into a third-century luxury city and explore it at will. On my visit, I encountered a larger-than-life statue of an angel—complete with wings. *What is this doing here?* I thought. This was a pagan city. There were no Christian angels here when it was abandoned. Then I realized why it was there and why Christian angels were depicted with wings. The messengers of the gods of Rome had to move from Mount Olympus to where they were sent. They had wings! The Greek word for *messenger* is *angelos*—angels. When Christians asked them to paint angels, they naturally painted them as they understood from past history. If, for example, you went to England and asked an artist to draw a football halfback, they would draw what we call a soccer player. Football is the name the Europeans call their game. The Gospel of Mark tells of a young man being at the empty tomb, whereas the Gospels of Matthew and Luke speak of angels. There is no contradiction. Mark simply identifies the messenger as a young man, while the others use the term *angelos*. I recalled that the mosaic in Ravenna, Italy, that depicted Abraham entertaining angels showed the angels as having no wings. Use the Ockham's razor approach, and that answer should satisfy the curious.

In my first book, *Can You Make the Buttons Even*, I devoted an entire chapter to this subject. I tell of encounters with angels who helped shape my life and the lives of others.

Church: Visible and Invisible

The idea that the church is composed of both a physical and a spiritual body is a long-accepted one. We speak of this as either the church visible or the church invisible. There is the obvious physical church complete with a building,

Sunday worship, staff, and bank account. Membership—or attendance—in one is the basis for calling oneself a Christian. The Church Invisible contains those whom I think of as followers of Christ. Some of them may have abandoned the Church Visible as being irrelevant to them. They are drawn together spiritually—wherever they are. They are the ones actively following the example and teachings of Jesus even if they do not recognize that fact. Fortunately, a section of the Church Invisible seems to reside in most congregations. They are the ones who reach out into the greater community to give help where help is needed. They are the ones pushing for social justice. They are the reason that the Church Visible continues to exist.

The term *ecclesiastical* refers to an established church; it comes from two Greek words: *ek* (out) and *kaleo* (I call). The literal meaning is "called out." That was the early church's understanding of itself. As a church of God, they were the ones called out to serve. That self-understanding is an essential part of any attempt at renewal. The hymns and final benediction can help with that. They can convey the thought of going forth to serve God by serving God's children.

SECTION 7

So Where Now?

Diagnosis always is easier than prescription. One can analyze what already exists. We can trace origin and decisive factors in the shaping of what already is. Prescription, the attempting to proscribe a cure or acceptable course of action, is more difficult. My purpose in writing this was largely diagnostic. I wanted to show the original message of the Christian faith and help the reader understand how it strayed from that redemptive, empowering message. Many good and brilliant men in the first few centuries developed theories to explain what they believed were critical questions of the faith. Scripture had not yet been declared as authoritative, so it is understandable that these brilliant minds drew from the understanding of their culture to formulate their doctrines. In doing so, however, they often formulated doctrines that were not only nonbiblical but were, in some cases, contrary to the teachings of Scripture. The most glaring is the doctrine of atonement. To the church's credit, they never approved atonement as an official doctrine. However, it has managed to slip into a central part of the church's thinking.

Along the way, many popular ideas developed that were nonbiblical. Many of these were natural results of the church's reversion to legalism. Annulment is one of the better-known teachings of this ilk. Biblical inerrancy is undoubtedly the most troublesome.

I believe there are many others with greater imaginations and a higher level of energy to address the prescription in detail. I will attempt a few suggestions, however, based upon my personal observations, reflections, and experience.

I believe the original message is summed up in the opening of Mark. Jesus begins his ministry with these words: *"The Kingdom of God is at hand. Repent and believe the good news."* The Greek for *Kingdom of God* literally means "nation of God." However, the first English translation was made in England—not the United States. There is a tendency for us Americans to envision something like Disney's Magic Kingdom—complete with castles—when we hear that phrase. The British, however, merely think in terms of a nation. I believe Jesus was simply saying that one did not have to wait for some future apocalyptic moment for God's kingdom to arrive. Rather, it was available for anyone at that moment. It called for a radical transformation of the mind. *Repent* literally in Greek means is *metanoia*—from *meta* (transformation as in *metamorphous*) and *noia* (not of body but of mind).

Radically transform the way you think, and you will be living as God's people—not Caesar's. Matthew does a magnificent job of laying out the essential approach in his Sermon on the Mount. I sometimes refer to that as the Christian Manifesto, for it clearly shows the radical difference in the value system of human society and God's society. I suggest that any serious study of our faith begin with an in-depth study of the Sermon on the Mount. Try to understand why Jesus says those who live by God's values are more blessed (more content, more at peace with themselves, and therefore genuinely happier in the deeper, truer sense than those who succeed by society's values).

As you read through Matthew, note the tone and message of each parable, each teaching. I believe you will see that a major theme is God's relentless love for his children. Another is that we are being called to fullness of life. Jesus does not call us to be saved from our sins. Jesus invites us to become more fully engaged in a selfless sharing of ourselves. He crosses the boundaries of exclusiveness to make inclusiveness a way of life. Another major theme is Jesus's disdain for—and struggle against—legalistic religion. His statement that "the Sabbath was made for man, man was not made for the Sabbath" (Mark 2:27) reveals a grasp of the purpose of religious faith rarely understood. For example, it has been said that "more than Israel has kept the Sabbath, the Sabbath has kept Israel." Genuine religious faith never restricts worthy human behavior. It helps draw people into a more harmonious relationship with creation. The Jewish Sabbath is a time for reflection upon one's life and one's relationship with creation and its purpose. Frankly, we lost something of value when we as a people allowed Sunday to become just another day of the week. Of course, long before it had faded into just another day, it had taken on the hue of joyless legalism. It had become a restriction rather than an enhancement of life. Many so-called Blue Laws were related to Sabbath—or Sunday for Christians—activities.

In your reflections or discussions of these essays, you would do well to ponder why this dynamic occurs. A joyful, liberating, and empowering spirit that was part of the founder's personality and flowed contagiously among early believers, eventually settled into some form of joyless control. It may help understand the present widening schism in the church between those who live in the old paradigm and those who live in the new.

Throughout the Gospel accounts, Jesus demonstrated the nature of his calling from God. He heals, he teaches, he comforts, and he feeds. He does not spend time talking about some future afterlife. He is concerned with issues of equality, justice, and unity. He speaks not of retribution but of reconciliation. He calls his followers to avoid violent confrontation and to overcome evil with loving response. Matthew 25:31 appears to sum up the requirements for any contemporary follower of Jesus. It is the ability to extend oneself for the well-being of another—any other person—without regard for who that person is. There is no suggestion that a Christian should ever employ violence for any purpose.

Jesus does not call the people sinners but tells them about their loving heavenly Father. By implication, the listeners are God's beloved children. How early theologians could miss this is beyond me. Jesus also tells the people they are the light of the world and calls for them to let their lights shine. When he is crucified, there is no suggestion that his followers were anything but devastated. No one felt closer to God because Jesus atoned for their sins.

Our dilemma lies in our humanity—our human nature. In this physical life, the physical, human dimension of life is more pressing than our spiritual dimension. We think in terms of immediate gratification of needs and desires. The long journey is not in our awareness. The values of our society (e.g., pleasure, security, privilege, power) are far more important and real than such attributes as contentment or deep-seated satisfaction. We spend a large portion of our lives pursuing society's goal before we mature to the point of even considering the alternatives. A few arrive at this stage in their thirties. Some stumble across it at an earlier age. However, the forties and fifties seem to be the age at which the average person begins to consider an alternative lifestyle.

So what can the emerging church do to change the flow of faith from dependence to independence, from self-seeking to joyful servanthood? I believe the essence of what we call original sin is egocentricity. We naturally begin to develop our ego around age two. A strong ego is essential for a healthy, autonomous adult. We need to know our personal boundaries: where we begin and where others end and vice versa, or we may become a figment of someone else's imagination. We need a strong sense of our values and goals, or we are easily led astray. In the course of developing our egos, we become—as a matter of course—egocentric. There are degrees of egocentricity ranging from healthy to destructive. However, every act we would call sinful has egocentricity as its source. The extremes are obvious: racism, sexism, any form of prejudice that rests upon differences of any types springs from our egocentricity. The less something resembles ourselves, the less desirable it is.

Lesser degrees of egocentricity may be manifested in bad driving habits—including road rage, running through traffic lights and signs, cutting into traffic rather than waiting for one's turn, discourteous public behavior—and language, cheating, stealing, lying, and demeaning others. At its extreme, it is narcissism and other sociopathic behavior. Sexual assault always is a manifestation of egocentricity.

Have I made my case? Please consider this fully. The need to lessen this egocentricity is obvious. This is the primary reason we must switch the focus of our faith from personal salvation to servanthood.

Here are a few suggestions:

1. Do not introduce children to the stories of the books of the Old Testament (Jewish Bible) until they are in high school. The central deity presented is a god of war with a need for vengeance. Instead, immerse them in the stories and teachings of Jesus and the current church at its best. Let them understand the loving, nurturing nature of God before introducing them to the earlier quest for understanding we find in the Old Testament books.
2. Demand lengthy membership orientation classes so that new members have a thorough understanding of the expectations of membership. This orientation should explain that Christians make a difference in society. Help new members to find a specific way in which they will carry out this mission.

3. Develop a system that will hold them accountable for their personal mission activities.
4. Develop a series of nearby mission programs where members can participate in a group activity.
5. Find ways to continually celebrate the ministries of the congregation.
6. Develop a liturgy that emphasizes the positive, empowered dimension of our faith.
7. The Methodist movement was powered by hymns. Hymns touch a part of us that mere words cannot. I usually spend at least a half hour selecting hymns that supported the morning's theme. I believe the opening hymn should have a sense of celebration and set the tone for the service. The final hymn should usually have a sense of sending forth.

A Final Word about Values, Principles, and Law

This is the underlying purpose of these essays. It deserves a final comment.

I mentioned earlier that there is a significant difference between a principle, a value, and a law. Jesus taught principles and values—never law. Yet the church quickly developed what they call canon law, and the church has been governed by this for centuries. Jesus's teachings are best understood as containing enduring principles and values that can be translated and acted upon in any culture. "Turn the other cheek," "go the extra mile," "love your neighbor as yourself" are not legalistic statements. They carry principles and values that shape the actions of those who would be followers of Jesus. Moral principles cannot be broken any more than a physical law can. We either learn them and abide by them or we create a problem for ourselves and possibility for others. The same could be said for values. There are an unlimited number of values—some useful, some destructive. Each of us is free to create our own value system. What I have observed and what Scriptures contend is that those with worthy values tend to have more contented and fulfilling lives. They have a positive attitude toward life and toward all living things.

I have seen far too many mean-spirited people whose lives developed from faulty value systems. They are more envious of the success of others, less able to enter into fruitful discussions of differences, and more fearful than the average person. They may give the impression of being macho and courageous, but beneath the surface, they are fearful. They do not do much for building a harmonious, cooperative community. Oh yes, they may be decent, law-abiding citizens who know and practice the basic courtesies; however, they rarely are truly friendly, and genuine intimacy is difficult for them.

Scripture says we have been made in the image of God. Jesus came to show us how to become the fulfillment of that image. We do not attain this level by merely discussing the issues. Ultimately, we must incorporate those qualities within ourselves. The task is continuous. There is no place we can stop and say we have arrived. However, that is why God has given us an eternity. In whatever phase of existence lies beyond this, we enter with only who we have become as our resource.

These are a few of the spiritual values that the church can assist in discovering and cultivating. This, I believe, is a main purpose for the church: to move people into a closer spiritual relationship with the God of Jesus Christ.

Spirit of Generosity

It is obvious that Jesus wanted to foster a spirit of generosity in his followers. His parables overflowed with that theme. The Good Samaritan was a generous spirit. The other two, even though Jewish, were not admirable people. The good shepherd whose sheep had strayed ventured forth, giving himself to locate and save the sheep. The waiting father of the prodigal son was a generous spirit. The moment his son returned, he only wanted to celebrate and share his joy. When his listeners were hungry, Jesus could have ended the session and sent them home. Instead, he chose to feed them. When a person needed his attention, he gave it. He was generous with his gifts and himself. The early followers of Jesus searched for abandoned children to bring into their homes. When a newcomer joined the community, they contributed whatever they possessed, and then the entire community shared with them. No one was caught up in the need to possess or to not give of themselves.

In my workshops, I find that people often have the fondest memories for those gifts they have given rather than for those they received. The exception being that it was a treasured gift from their early childhood days.

Today's followers of Jesus need to cultivate that same spirit of generosity. This ability to give oneself is an essential attribute of spiritual maturity. There are many ways of fostering this. Contemporary Christians need to find those ways.

Spirit of Empathy

One may be generous but not care for the recipient. It is one thing to give your resources to aid someone. It is another to actually care about the recipient. Charity today often is expressed by dropping a few dollars into a kettle or simply using a credit card in response to a mailed solicitation. The original translation of the Greek term for *love* (*agape*) was *charity*. However, people began to say they did not want someone's charity (because it was too dispassionate), so the translators arbitrarily changed the word to *love*. The term actually denotes the ability and willingness to extend oneself for the well-being of another.

When our battalion redeployed to Japan in the early '50s, I could speak a bit of Japanese, so I was appointed as community relations officer. One project we took on was to build new showers for a nearby orphanage. Whenever I would drive into their parking lot, I was met by a hoard of children, shouting the name of our unit (999) and wanting hugs. I quickly set myself up with pockets full of candy and Kleenex (it was winter, and noses ran). I soon developed a fondness for those children. I cared about them and how they were housed and fed and educated. I suppose I could have been "all business" and only relate to the headmaster, but that was not to be. Their greeting and my hugging them, wiping noses, and handing out candy were the highlight of the entire trip. Empathy! It is the foundation for relationships.

I know I have empathy with a person when I honestly rejoice at their success. There is no sense of envy or having lost out in some way. Empathy is stronger and has more depth than mere compassion.

Spirit of Community

A spirit of community carries a tacit awareness of a covenant. People in a community have an unwritten contract as to how they will behave. They treat one another with courtesy—wherever they are—including traffic. They obey the laws and do not push for special treatment.

Spirit of Generativity

Generativity is a term Erik Erikson uses to define a mature stage in life. He claims a person either develops generativity or stagnation. One strong aspect of generativity is the desire to pass along a worthy future to ensuing generations, whereas stagnation becomes self-absorbed. Generativity expresses itself various ways. It may range from mentoring children to endowing scholarships. Generativity is productive in some way. We all have witnessed mature people who personify generativity as well as those who have stagnated and seemed only hanging around, waiting to die. No one consciously chooses to become the latter. They just allowed it to happen to them.

Hopefully, these essays have given you fresh insights into this thing we call Christianity. I sincerely believe that a greater understanding of the reality of our faith enhances our ability to live our lives more fully and worthily. If this resonates with you, share that with your pastor. A worthy reformation can begin wherever there is a well-educated pastor who knows there is support for his/her genuine understandings. I believe we are called to be companions for God. We have been made in God's (spiritual) image. Our life purpose is to grow into the fullness of that image as seen in Jesus Christ. The original message of Jesus called the people into a spiritual relationship with God. That message still is valid where there is courage and commitment.

Perhaps it is proper to end this brief presentation with the words used by Dr. Albert Schweitzer, renowned French-German philosopher, theologian, and humanitarian. He was awarded the Nobel Prize in 1952 for his work on *Reverence for Life*. He also was an outstanding organist whose interpretation of Bach influenced many. On a trip to Africa, he had experienced a life-transforming moment of insight that caused him to quit his post as professor, go to medical school, and then spend the remainder of his life as a medical missionary in Africa. He gained further renown by writing *The Quest for the Historic Jesus*. His monumental groundbreaking work finally deduced that Scripture had too many myths, legends, and unwarranted additions to be able to fully identify the man of Galilee whom we call the Christ.

So in his conclusion to that work, he invited the readers to make their own search for the risen Christ.

> He comes to us as one unknown, as of old he came to those by the seaside who knew him not. He speaks the same words, 'Follow me,' and sets us to the tasks he has to fulfill for our time. He commands, and to those who obey him, whether they be wise or simple, he will reveal himself in the toils, the conflicts, the struggles we shall pass through in his fellowship. And as in an inexpressible mystery they shall come to know in their own experience who he is.

Blessings on your journey.
Richard Cheatham, March 1, 2018

Made in the USA
Middletown, DE
24 April 2018